What people are saying.

The House on Poland Hill

"Kathryn Cain's novel The House on Poland Hill is a good read! If you like stories of haunted houses and Greek Mythology, this book is for you."
Melissa French, Indianapolis, Indiana

Poet Tree, an Anthology of Short Stories and Poems by Kathryn Cain and Steven Cain, featuring, JD Widgery

"What a wonderful collection of unique, fascinating short stories. All different, all remarkable, and all with a unique twist at the end. Hard to put down. From tales of farm life to Syfy, all rolled into a package of compelling pieces that quickly carries the reader from one to the next."
Greg Lamp, St. Paul, Minnesota

"Wow, your stories are wildly imaginative and really get you thinking in the abstract. Melissa describes them as "brief, poignant, and fantastical. They cause you to ponder reality and sometimes feel as if a dream has come to life. They are very entertaining and nicely sized morsels of fiction. I would read one or two at a time as a brief distraction during my work day".
Ted and Melissa Maillett, Vienna, Virginia

The Prophecy

"I read Cain's The Prophecy in one sitting. Once I started, I couldn't put it down! The novel seems to take inspiration from the great Stephen King, but is certainly not lacking her own personal style and originality. I am looking forward to Cain's next work!"
Jasmine Widgery, Seattle, Washington

The Uniting of Harverness

"A Captivating read from start to finish. This novel takes you along on the spell-binding journey of Lady Elizabeth Elinor Lucrite—Princess of Harverness, through foreign lands and moments of fear and wonder as she seeks to avoid an alliance being forced upon her. The decision to walk away from all that is familiar and remain true to herself serves to remind us there is no reward without risk and sometimes a leap of faith. Kathryn Cain does an amazing job weaving the characters and the story to keep you riveted to the last page."
Brenda Vaught, Lafayette, Indiana

Simon Hunter

"Enchanting. Another winner from Kathryn Cain. In this new novel, she takes a seemingly ordinary small-town couple on a magical adventure. I was hooked from the start and couldn't predict a single twist or turn. This enchanting book makes heroes out of regular people – I highly recommend it!"
Sherry French Miller, Apple Valley, Minnesota

The Wolf, A Daniel Wolfgang Frasier Adventure

"Kathryn Cain has found her genre in The Wolf. An unexpected romp through the realms of the supernatural, every surprise, held me captive. I found myself rooting for characters and then reconsidering my loyalties when secrets were revealed. I await Dan's next adventure with bated breath."
Debbie French-Allbright- Oxford, Ohio

The House on Poland Hill

By Kathryn Cain

Books by Upon The Moment Publishing, LLC

UPON THE
MOMENT
PUBLISHING

TM

Upon The Moment Publishing, LLC

From Novelist Kathryn Cain

   The Prophecy, Copyright © 2021

   The Uniting of Harverness, Copyright© 2021

   Simon Hunter, Copyright© 2022

   The Wolf, A Daniel Wolfgang Frasier Adventure, Copyright© 2023

   The House on Poland Hill, Copyright© 2024

From Novelist Steven Cain

   Sunset Kings, Copyright© 2020

   The Accident in Larson, Copyright © 2021

   War At Home, Copyright© 2022

   Bets & Breakfasts, Copyright© 2023

   Criminal Liaisons, Copyright© 2024

From the minds of Kathryn Cain, Steven Cain, and JD Widgery

   Poet Tree, An Anthology of Short Stories and Poems, Copyright©2024

The House on Poland Hill, Copyright © 2024 by Upon the Moment

Publishing, LLC, Kathryn Cain

UPON THE
MOMENT
PUBLISHING   TM

Cover Design created by Stephanie Cain

Library of Congress Control Number: 2025903053

ISBN: **979-8-9924876-1-9**   Paperback   **$12.00**

ISBN: **979-8-9924876-2-6**   E-Book $ 4.00

I dedicate this novel, The House on Poland Hill, to my son Jason David Widgery, who lived at the top of Poland Hill, which inspired this story. Jason passed away on March 30, 2024—a beloved man who died way too soon. I spoke of this book long before I was able to begin it. I had a few in front, perhaps. Jason knew it was coming. I wish I had finished it before he left this world. He saw our anthology come to life, The Poet Tree, before he passed into his new life. It includes works of his own. So to you, my dear son Jason, this one's for you. All my love, Ma.

The House on Poland Hill

UPON THE
MOMENT
PUBLISHING ™

Chapter One

Everyone has heard of that house. You know the one I mean. The big one. The one that sits on top of the hill and overlooks the town. The haunted one, steeped in rummers and whisperings. Yes, that's the one. Well, I bought it last year at the beginning of fall. It had been my goal since childhood, and I also thought it was a remarkable financial deal. I may have been wrong.

I met the realtor on that warm, fateful day in September. The sun shone brightly between the tree leaves, which caused a flashing effect in my eyes and made my head cringe, a result of photophobia – I'm afraid, as I drove up the long, winding lane named Poland Hill Road, which led to the house from town. I passed through the large, black, wrought iron gate, which stood open for the first time. I stopped, shifted it to neutral, and pulled the brake lever. Leaving the auto door open, I exited and walked over to the humongous yet delicately and intricately engraved gate. Just for a brief second, I touched it with my right index finger. "Whew," I whispered under my breath. I got back in the car and took off. My eyes widened as I rounded the last curve of the lane and saw the mansion in its entirety for the first time in my life. One prominent bronze spire rose above the tree line and was the only part visible to the town below.

She awaited by the door on the top step as I arrived. Donning a big yellow dress with a matching hat, she was the proverbial Southern Woman. An unseasonably bright dress for a day in September. The brightness of the vast yellow fabric enhanced the headache the staccato sunshine had started. She waved eagerly at me as I pulled up before the steps. I half expected a white cotton glove to encase her hand. But there was none. Somehow, that was a relief. I put the gear shift into first gear and shut it off. I glanced in the rearview mirror, brushed my brown, wavy hair back in place with my fingers, and flattened the ascot around my neck. I grabbed my gold eagle-headed black cane from the floorboard beside me and exited my cherry red, sparklingly clean Mercedes-Benz AMG GT C Roadster.

I walked around the back of the Roadster and flashed my best grin. I stepped onto the first step and double-tapped the gold-headed cane on the concrete while extending my hand to her. We met halfway in the middle of the steps. I took her hand in mine and lifted it for a quick buss with my lips.

"Mrs. Wintergreen, how delightful you look today." I looked up at her with my brilliant blue eyes, glancing over the hand still grasped within mine. "What a perfect garment color choice to show off your refreshingly sunkissed cheeks." I flattered her, released her hand ceremoniously, and bowed with a flourish. "Enchanté."

"Why, Mr. Prescott," she fanned herself with her newly released fingers, "you are the sweetest man."

"Oh, call me Alistair, please," I declared, holding my arm out to her.

We turned and proceeded up the giant concrete steps together. I looked up at the house which loomed before us. The sun sparkled, bouncing against the lead windows, preventing any glimpse of the mansion's interior. It was a formidable sight, this house. I had purchased it only for its reputation. Of course, I had heard the tales and had seen the top of the most prominent sparkling spire from the town below, but I had only once set foot upon the road that had led me here.

"I am sorry I didn't attend your closing. I was quite surprised you purchased it this morning, sight unseen," Mrs. Wintergreen continued. "I should have thought you would at least want to see the grounds first."

"Oh, quite," I responded. "I have heard the tales about it, haven't I? One cannot grow up here and not know the grounds cover most of the hill itself. I have known what the property entails for a long time, my dear. Besides, I arrived in town only one day before the closing. Thursday, as it happens. I made all the arrangements through my attorney before arriving to sign the final paperwork this morning. I was so pleased the title company had an opening due to a cancellation on a Friday morning. I am quite sure that does not happen frequently."

Mrs. Wintergreen giggled unseemly. I could not help but wince at the screeching sound of it. "Why, of course, Alistair. I am aware of your late arrival. How I would have entertained you if you had arrived a weekend earlier." She batted her eyelashes sweetly in my direction.

I was terrified to know what she was going on about. We continued up the concrete steps, and as she held my arm for support, I could not help but glance at the land sprawling around me. The most magnificent pines, majestic Palmetto, and huge gnarly Southern Live Oaks, whose arms seemed to stretch forever across the vast expanse of land, surrounded the immense grounds. My mind began to wander.

The house, a large mansion actually, sat vacant atop Poland Hill for what seemed an eternity. It was at its heyday, so the story was told, in the roaring twenties. It had been a grand, albeit small, hotel, with parties galore, hot spas for health treatments, and a movie cinema, which was said to show the first talkie, The Jazz Singer, in 1927. Of course, it would not have been complete without a horse track for betting and an amusement park with a steam-powered carousel hidden deep within the forest behind the hotel—a hotel that catered only to the rich and the famous.

In 1934, after scores of deaths due to a massive, rampant fire, the owners shut down the entire property, including the hotel, amusement park, and race track. It sat vacant for many years. Nearly thirty years later, it was purchased by an old man named Wilbur Hamilton. Word had it he was a descendant of Alexander Hamilton. The mansion was left to rot all those years, but Mr. Hamilton had the good fortune to find it in nearly perfect repair. It took him only two years to return it to its original beauty. Rumor had it even the beautiful original burgundy carpets were spared. I found it difficult to believe for years after I heard this story. But if I had convinced myself the stories about the house on Poland Hill were true, I should not have accepted this rumor as anything but truth.

I had heard the story all of my life. Curiosity had gotten the better of me when, at twelve years old, a couple of my friends and I decided to take matters into our own hands and see firsthand what this fine manse had to offer. We waited until our parents settled down after dinner in front of the evening's television programs and slipped out to meet on our bikes at the end of our road. The summer sun was still high in the sky, and we could see the old building's spire rising on the hilltop in the distance above us. Even then, the sun glinted from the leaded windows. It seemed a beacon, beckoning us to come, see, and witness the truth of its secrets.

"Hey, Tommy," I called out as I skidded to a stop. Dry gravel road dust fluffed up around my ankles. "This is great. Did you have any trouble getting out of the house?"

"Not at all, Ali," Tommy answered. "My parents drank so much wine at dinner they didn't even want to watch television. They just told me they were going to bed early." He laughed out loud, "You know what that means."

Frankie burst out laughing, "Indubitably, I know what it means, butt head." He bent over and held his gut, one hand still locked firmly to his bike to keep it from falling over.

"Yes, Tommy, I know what it means," I answered. "But don't call me Ali. It sounds like a girl's name. You know I don't like it." Even though it was precisely what my parents always called me.

Tommy stopped laughing, "Yah, yah. I know, Ali. It's just a habit. It's what I have always called you. Sorry, Alistair." He removed his ball cap and bowed at the waist, "Yes Sir, Mr. Alistair Prescott, Sir."

"Funny, Tommy." I was not amused. I looked over at Frankie. He was a chubby little kid with red curly hair and bright green eyes. He wore a red and black striped shirt, which reminded me of Freddie Krueger, and he had big scabs on both pale knees. Tommy's comment aside, I couldn't help but laugh when I looked at him, still in the thralls of his laughter. He was my friend. He was a chubby, funny, leaky guy, but my friend, nonetheless.

Frankie finally stood straight, tears of laughter streaming down his fat cheeks. "That's a good one, Tommy," He spat with his chuckling. "I don't even want to think of my parents doing anything like that."

Then his laughter exploded, and he doubled over again. After his laughter subsided, he looked at Tommy, "Hey, maybe we should start calling you Thomas? What do you think?" Then he doubled over again.

"Get a grip, Frankie," I said, smiling. "I want to get up to the top as fast as possible." I looked up at the dark manse with the shiny windows and couldn't wait any longer to get started.

Tommy and I jumped on our bikes and raced as quickly as we could around the corner onto the next road. We left Frankie behind in our wake of dust.

"Wait up, guys," he called. "Don't go without me."

We could hear him grunt as he lugged his chubby, round body onto the seat and chugged loudly behind us. Tommy and I looked at each other and smiled, his brown eyes tearing up with laughter, but we stopped, held up, and waited for him to catch up with us. He was our friend, after all.

We rode like the Three Musketeers, together in a row, down our road toward Main Street. When we hit the main road through town, we skidded to the side of the northbound lane and stopped to catch our breath. We each pulled our water canteens out of our backpacks and slugged some down. One would think it couldn't get this hot in Prophet, South Carolina, but going on 7:00 p.m., it was still hovering just under 90 degrees. Dust covered us from the lack of rain, and my lower legs began to itch.

"Wow, Frankie," I said. "Slow down with the chugging. We haven't even started the hill climb yet. The water has to last us until we get back home." I admonished. "I mean, I don't plan to be gone all night," I looked over at Tommy, who nodded his agreement. "But I want to hang out when we get there for a while. You know, check out the sights and stuff."

Frankie pulled his bottle hesitantly from his lips. His pale face flushed from exertion, but he nodded his understanding and agreement to our pact to explore the hotel this evening.

"Sure, Alister. I get it," he agreed. He tucked his canteen back into his backpack and wiped his hand across his face. He seemed to dry his lips and his nose with the same motion. "Let's get going then," he said, although he still panted a bit.

I signaled the go-ahead, and the three of us left the roadside to head north. Main Street led us straight to Poland Hill Road. Oddly enough, the road was called Poland Hill Road. Go figure. So much for creativity, I thought. But then the name worked for all intents and purposes. I mean, everyone knew where Poland Hill Road would lead, right?

It took us over half an hour to reach three-fourths of the way to the top of Poland Hill. We paused to get a quick drink of water and breathed a collective sigh of relief that we were almost there. We took off with eager excitement and came around a curve. A huge Wrought iron fence blocked the entire width of the road. We skidded to a stop in the loose gravel, and I was sure Tommy would slide right into the massive gate. But he didn't.

"Whew, that was a rush," Tommy said. He laid his bike down in the gravel and brushed the dust off his shins. "I thought I was a goner there." He laughed and glanced around while we quietly waited on our bikes, scoping the land around us. "Guys," Tommy said curiously, "take a look around."

Frankie and I dropped our bikes onto the gravel at our feet and joined Tommy in the middle of the road. We looked around us. The pines had seemed to surround us unannounced while we had biked uphill. We concentrated all our senses on our bikes, legs, lungs, and exertion as we biked, not on the sights or the scents around us.

We gazed at those large pines and realized they had completely blocked the sun. Poland Hill Road was darker here, darker than Main Street in town. We quieted and listened to the sounds that grew suddenly around us. I could hear crickets chirping, birds squawking, and the long call of a coyote in the soft breeze. Why would a coyote be here, on this hill, in the middle of town? I glanced at Tommy and Frankie to see if they felt the same chill I suddenly felt in the air. I brushed my brown wavy hair back from my forehead, and my fingers felt sweat clinging there. Was this sweat from the exertion up the hill, or was this the sweat from something else? Was this fear, perhaps? All the hair on my arms and neck stood up straight. Heck, I could even feel the hairs on my legs stand at attention. What did I need to pay attention to, I wondered. I rubbed my arms against the chill and lifted my nose to the overwhelming fragrance of pine lingering in the air.

"Hey, Ali," Tommy whispered. "Do you feel what I feel?" he asked.

"Yeah, Tom, I do," I didn't care, in that moment, that he had called me Ali.

Frankie moved closer to get in between us. "What is going on, guys?" he asked. "How could it get so cold so fast? I mean, it was what? Was it eighty-five degrees thirty minutes ago? What do you think it is now?"

"It was closer to ninety," I corrected him, "but it feels like it's in the fifties right now," I said, looking up at the sky above the top of the pines. It could not be dark yet, but the pines did more than block out the sun. The sun's rays didn't even reach the sky above them. It was only seven-thirty and shouldn't get dark at this time of year until much later.

"Look at the fence, Alister," Tommy said, his voice betraying a hint of frailty.

I pulled my attention away from the top of the pines and tried to spy on him in the growing darkness. He leaned over with his hand against the iron fence.

"What's up with the fence, Tommy?" I didn't know and couldn't see what he was talking about.

"Look at this gate. It's so big. It's got a huge lock and chain sealing it closed." Tommy jiggled the massive lock with both hands. The lock rattled against the iron gate with loud clangs. "There is no way we are going to get it opened." He dropped the lock, and it banged sharply and sounded like an explosion. Frankie and I both covered our ears in a flash.

"Geesh, Tommy," Frankie complained. "Did you have to do that?"

"Way to go, man," I said, the clang still ringing in my ears.

Tommy looked admonished but went on, "Look at the fence. The bars are so close together we can't even squeeze between them." He gestured toward Frankie, "especially him."

Frankie groaned. "Thanks a lot, man."

"Well, it's true, isn't it?"

"Maybe, but you don't have to rub it in, dog face." Frankie's face turned more red than it had been, and I hoped he wouldn't pop a blood vessel.

"Guys," I said, "let's see if there is any other way in there." I took a second look at that massive gate. The scrollwork and engraved designs covering the entire gate, as well as the fence, were beautifully crafted. It almost looked like some ancient writing or something on them. For some reason, my mind thought of a chant.

"Why is it so dark here, Alister?" Frankie turned east, his hand trailing over the fence posts as if looking for a hidden gate or something.

"I don't know, Frankie," I answered honestly. I had no idea. It didn't seem scientifically possible. I couldn't wrap my mind around it either. The dimness of the light and the feel of the air didn't sit quite right with me.

I walked up to the fence that was attached to the gate and looked up. It was at least three feet above my head. I glanced at Tommy, who had moved west to scout the fence in that direction. I glanced east at Frankie. Both boys were running their hands over the iron as they followed the enclosure to the tree lines. I reached out and touched the metal. I jumped back a foot and rubbed my hand against my chest. Electric shock! How could that be? Frankie and Tommy were touching it. I reached out, braced myself, and felt it with one fingertip. It zapped so hard I thought I could hear my skin sizzle. I stuck my finger in my mouth and tasted something. Ozone? Burnt flesh? Weird.

"Hey, guys," I yelled, a little too spookily. "Come back here." True friends, they ran back in a flash.

"What's up, Alister?"

"What do you want?"

"Did you guys feel anything when you touched the fence?"

"Like what?" They both asked at the same time.

"Like, did you get shocked or anything? Feel a buzz or something?"

"From the fence?" Frankie eyed me curiously.

"Why do you think we would get shocked, Ali? I didn't feel anything," Tommy looked at Frankie, "Did you feel anything, Frankie?"

"No, nothing." Frankie answered, "Did you feel something, Alister?"

I lifted my right hand and showed them my finger. Even in the dim light, they could see it was bright red and starting to blister.

"Wow, what happened, Alister?" Tommy grabbed my finger and pulled it closer to him. "What did you do?"

I pulled my hand out of his grasp. "I touched the fence," I whispered. "That's all I did. I saw you guys running your hands all over the fence, but when I touched it, it shocked me."

The guys looked at each other and smiled. "Sure, right, Ali," Tommy said. "That's a good one. How did you get your finger so red? What did you do to get your finger to blister?"

"I'm telling you the truth, Tom." I was indignant. "Why would I lie about it? I grabbed the metal post and jumped a mile. I saw you both touching it just fine. So I touched it again. First, it was a small shock, and then it fried my finger." I held my finger up again so they could look at it.

"Neato," Frankie said. "Touch it again, and let me see."

"You are an idiot, Frankie," Tommy laughed and ruffled Frankie's red hair. "Why would he want to do it again if what he said is true?"

Frankie couldn't help but laugh. "Well, I thought it sounded like a good idea." He looked at me, "Sorry, Alister. You don't have to touch it again."

"That's great, Frankie, because I wouldn't anyway." It surprised me that he wanted me to harm myself to prove what happened to me. I knew he was a dufus, but that was ridiculous.

"Why would it shock you but not us?" Tommy queried. He shook his head and walked closer to the iron fence. Tom briefly looked back at Frankie and me, then reached out and clasped his hand around a pole. He held it there for quite a while, then let go and walked back to us. "Nothing. I felt nothing, Ali." He shook his head. "I don't get it."

"Neither do I," I answered softly, running my eyes all over the gate. "Do you guys want to try to climb the fence and go in? I can wait here. You can tell me what you find in there." I heard the unveiled disappointment in my words. I had wanted to see inside for as long as I could remember.

The guys looked at each other and nodded.

"Great," I said excitedly. At least someone would see inside. "Let me help give you a step up, I said to Tommy. I thought Frankie might be a little too much for my muscles. I got as close to the fence as I dared and squatted down on my knees. Tommy eagerly climbed onto my shoulders.

"Ready," he almost giggled. "This is going to be great!" He reached out and grabbed onto the fence.

I was afraid the electricity would go right through his body and shock me anyway. But it didn't. This isn't how electricity is supposed to work.

Tommy got me moving. "Stand up, Alister. I can't reach the top." He stretched his back and arms as long and straight as possible but couldn't reach the fence's top.

"Okay, Tommy. Hold on," I grabbed onto his ankles, dangling at my waist, and tried to stand up without touching any metal.

It was tough. I thought my legs were strong, but they were suddenly wobbly. Frankie grabbed my elbow and helped pull me to my feet. Tommy could easily reach the top now. Frankie kept hold of my arm but put a hand up for Tommy to step onto, and Tom hoisted himself onto the fence top.

He slid his tennis shoe between two spikey-looking pole points and yelled, "Look at me! I made it." He shouted at the top of his lungs, "I'm the king of the gate! I made it first. I'm the greatest to have ever lived!" He pounded his chest like an ape. "I scaled the fence faster than Spider-Man!" I rolled my eyes as he raised his fist to the darkening sky. A flash of lighting immediately answered him.

The sky opened. Rain and hail poured down upon our heads. Blinded, Tommy nearly slipped from the top of the fence. The black iron visually appeared to tilt in an attempt to loosen him from his perch. I told myself it was just an illusion caused by the torrent and the hail, but I wasn't quite sure. I watched him, my mouth open in a silent gasp. The fence won. Tommy lost his footing and landed right at our feet, with a hard thud, on the rain-slicked mud.

He looked up at Frankie and me, eyes wide. Grass hung from his face, and mud dripped from his eyelashes. "Thanks a lot, guys," he was not happy. "You could have at least tried to catch me." He raised his voice loud enough for us to hear above the onslaught of rain and hail. He popped to his feet, mopped off his face as best he could with his forearm, and we all ran to our bikes. It was impossible to avoid the rain, so running was moot. We were already drenched.

Disappointment slammed down on us as we peddled back down Poland Hill Road as fast as possible. The rain and hail stopped as we reached the halfway mark down the hill. By the time we hit Main Street, it was almost 8:30 p.m., and the abnormal darkness had given way to the typical summer evening sky. The sun was beginning to slip out of view.

Main Street was dry. "You see that, guys?" I asked. "No rain or hail
here." I was mystified. "How could it get dark as night and storm only
up on top of Poland Hill? Surely, that isn't possible. I mean, I guess I
have seen a lone cloud rain down in the distance while I stood a few
miles away in the sunlight. But Poland Hill is smack dab in the center
of town." I couldn't see how it could happen. The hill was right above
us. I looked up at it and saw the sunlight etching the silhouettes of the
pines.

"That's too weird, Ali," Tom answered me. "I don't get it either."
He looked back and forth between Frankie and me as we sat perched
upon our dripping-wet bikes. "Unless the house really is haunted, and
it didn't want us to be there." His eyes grew wide, and he began
making an oohing sound. "Ooh, ooh, I am the ghost of Poland Hill. You
can not pass this way. You are forbidden." He raised his arms in a
Frankenstein fashion.

"You think so?" Frankie sounded spooked. "Do you really think it is
haunted?"

Tommy burst out laughing. "What do you think, Frankie?" He
almost fell off his bike as tears streamed from his eyes.

"Come on, guys." I hated always being the straight guy. "Frankie,
he's kidding. I guess it was just a weird anomaly of some scientific
weather phenomena. We can try again." My finger throbbed beneath
the blister, a reminder of my reaction to the wrought iron. I didn't

17

know how I was going to try again, yet as I looked up into the rain, I could glimpse the highest window in the spire, and it whispered to me. At that very moment, I knew I would buy the old mansion. Somehow, some way, I would buy it.

Tommy looked closely at us from perched on his bike, "Did you guys know that after the hotel fire, after it was closed for years, some old guy bought the place and lived there alone? He turned the darn thing into his home. What do you think about that? They say he's where the first ghost stories came from, from that old man. They say they had to carry him out on a stretcher. He was babbling all kinds of nonsense before he got his wits about him and started talking about ghosts. Well, I guess he didn't really have his wits about him." Tommy shrugged and giggled.

He finally pulled my attention from the rising spire, "I know all about it, Tommy," I answered automatically but felt my head caught up in a spot of rain. I had studied everything I could about this building. I never figured out why I was so intrigued.

"I didn't know that," Frankie shook his red curls back and forth. "How come I never knew about that?" He looked at us both. "Why are you only telling me this now? I guess I didn't know where the stories started."

"I don't know, Frankie. I guess we've never talked about that part of its history. But that isn't really quite right, though. The stories

18

started after the great fire. We just never heard them before they pulled him out of there, and the gossip spread through town." I wasn't sure why we had never talked about it before, but I had read books about that fire.

"I guess we better head home now. It's almost my 9:00 o'clock curfew." Frankie said, wiping his still-dripping hair from his eyes. "They'll croak if I'm not home in time."

"Sure, Frankie," Tom agreed. Tom and I have 10:00 p.m. curfews in the summertime. But our parents weren't Frankie's.

Frankie's parents are Charles and Betty Franklin. They named Frankie Franklin Franklin. Who does that? They treat him like he's still four years old. Maybe that's why he was a little blubbery sometimes. I get it.

We agreed to meet at about 9:00 a.m. the following morning and hang out. Maybe plan a revisit to Poland Hill Road. The three of us lived on the same street, and I looked behind us as we rode through the last remaining light. We left a trail of water in our wake. It didn't take us five more minutes to get home from the corner where our street met Main. I watched Tommy and Frankie enter their homes as I dropped my bike on my front lawn. I yelled "hello" as I banged in through the kitchen door and passed the dark living room. The television cast an eerie glow but was silent. They had left it on again.

The House on Poland Hill

I entered my bedroom, closed the door, and slipped off my soggy clothes. I draped them carefully over the heating grate so Mom wouldn't have a cow if she found them wet on the bedroom floor in the morning. I went to my dresser and pulled out a pair of skivvies, as my Dad called them, and a tee shirt. I pulled them on and slid into bed. I turned off the bedside lamp before remembering I hadn't stopped at the bathroom to brush my teeth. Oh, well. I pulled the bed covers up around my chin and lay there with my eyes open for the longest time. The house had gotten under my skin and wouldn't let go. I didn't know this was the first and only time the three of us would try to get into the house on Poland Hill together. I would not have fallen asleep so soon if I had known then.

Chapter Two

I followed Mrs. Wintergreen through the ten-foot-tall, double Mahogany doors she had already unlocked and stood ajar; a dull brass lock and hinges belied their recent buffing. I thought I would have to hire someone to correct that. I figured it would soon require many more repairs, but I was quite surprised to see the entry foyer was exquisite. The pale gray and white marble flooring showed hardly a bit of wear. It gleamed as if brand new, which was far different than the weathering of the brass on the outside of the door. I turned and moved the massively heavy doors to and fro behind me. There was not a sound as they moved. The brass on the inside was superb. My face reflected as if someone had recently polished them. I had made no such prior arrangement. The same hand had not polished the outside as had polished the inside; of this I was sure.

With a flourish and twirling her oversized yellow dress, Mrs. Wintergreen swirled and closed the door behind her as I studied my half. Interesting fact. Why would someone take the time to shine the inside but not the outside? I clucked my tongue and pulled my attention from the doors to Mrs. Wintergreen's chatter.

"Welcome, welcome, Mr. Alister," she prattled on as she swept her arms around the air in a gestured display of the room. "I am so sure you will be delighted with your purchase. You can look around and see what a beauty this building used to be. The prior owner did a wonderful job attempting to restore it to its original beauty. It is a shame he wasn't able to complete it." She pointed at the marble floor beneath our feet. "Just look at this beautiful marble. Hiring someone to buff it back to perfection shouldn't take much effort."

"Why, whatever do you mean, Mrs. Wintergreen?" I inquired. "It is gleaming the most brilliant sparkles of sunlight upon it. I should think it doesn't even need a mopping." She squinted her eyes in my direction. "I think it is more beautiful than I could or would have imagined after the building was closed for so long." I looked up at the massive hotel lobby before me. "Why, it does have a certain Je ne sais quoi, does it not?" My heart beat quickly at the beauty opening up before me.

"Mr. Alister, are you jesting with me?" She asked, perplexed. "I had hoped to have a cleaning team come in last week to attempt to make it ready for you, but alas," I was sure she was feeling faint, hand to her forehead and spittle slipping from her round, pink lips, "I could find no one who was even interested in attempting to clean it." Mrs. Wintergreen lowered her hand and swept across the floor to what appeared to be the front desk of this large establishment. "You know the tales, of course. None would accept what I believe was a generous offer to make it ready for you." She tutted. "But look at this beautiful front counter." Her hand ran haphazardly over the silken mahogany, which did, in fact, match the front doors. She rubbed her hands together as if soiled and said, "A little elbow grease, and you will have this looking shipshape in no time. I can't understand how it survived the fire at all. It looks like the prior owner didn't even attempt any repairs in this part of the hotel."

I walked over to where she stood and looked at the magnificent structure. I could see no dent or marking against its perfect face. "I don't understand, dear Mrs. Wintergreen. It looks perfectly maintained. Why, I don't even see a bit of dust in the corners or within the scrollwork on the sides." I slid my hand over the contours of the desk and felt the wood slide smoothly beneath my touch. "I don't know what you are talking about. It is a beauty to see." I turned to look at her and laughed with a sigh of relief. "It is quite remarkable, actually. I was sure it would be in a huge mess of ill repair." I spun on my heel and took in the one-hundred-foot-long lobby. Several floors rose above me, and the hallways on each floor formed a square around the entire building. I could glimpse the doors of the guest suites behind the brass balustrades surrounding each floor balcony— an attempt to keep the guests safe from plunging to their deaths. But stories told of one poor bloke who had too much drink and did precisely that.

I looked further. Scattered across the gray and white marble floors, marble pillars, each spanning a minimum of eight feet in diameter, trussed the ceiling. At least ten pillars held up the golden dome that had to be one hundred feet above my head. "Why, Mrs. Wintergreen, it is extraordinary." I found myself suddenly laughing at its sheer beauty. The sun shone through the most ornately decorated leaded windows and shattered prisms upon the marble floors, the golden and bronze decorative scrolling on the floors, walls, and trusses. The manse was indeed a place of time-forgotten glory, and my mind's eye could envision the wealthy patrons dallying upon lavish furniture, hands filled with golden glasses of champagne. I looked around the lobby and was thrilled to see what must have been the original furniture, all in pristine condition. What's this, three-seated leather lobby chairs placed near each truss pillar? How lavish! Several dark green stuffed sofas and chairs with golden tufts were paired in groupings about the space, cherry wood tables were within the groupings, and tall cherry wood tables were strewn about for standing guests—a purely ravishing display of glamour.

What if I hadn't purchased this place? What if that morning, when I woke up thinking I was meeting Tommy and Frankie, it didn't happen the way it had?

I rushed out of my room, pulling the shirt down over my head as I entered the kitchen, yelling out to my mother I was headed out to meet the guys when I stopped short at the kitchen doorway. Mom was pulling dishes from the cabinets, wrapping them in newspaper, and setting them into labeled boxes. My eyes widened in shock.

"What's going on, Mom?" I was afraid to ask. I didn't want to know what was going on. She continued to wrap dishes as she looked at me. It was a moment of silence save for the crumpling sounds of the paper. "Mom?" I hesitantly asked again.

"Alister," she answered, "Go ask your Father." With a brush off, she turned back to pull more plates from the shelf.

I said nothing back to her as I ran from the kitchen and out into the dooryard. Dad was moving the living room couch into a trailer. I ran up to him and stopped abruptly. I started to feel my heart run away inside of my chest. Was I going to have a panic attack? I had had one once before when I was small. I thought it would never happen again, but here it was, my chest suddenly unable to expand to draw in even the slightest breath.

Dad looked over at me, staring at him struggling with the sofa. "Look here, Ali, come give us a hand, will you?" He asked in his clipped British accent.

I hurried over to help him, still struggling for breath. "What's up, Dad?" I gripped the end of the sofa and helped him push it up into the back of the trailer.

Dad pulled his red handkerchief from his back pocket and mopped his brow. It was already eighty degrees at 9:00 a.m. He leaned against the back of the trailer and looked at me.

"Dad?" I asked again.

"We wanted to wait, Ali. We didn't want to tell you until the last minute." He tucked his handkerchief into his back pocket and smoothed back his wavy blond hair from his damp brow.

"Didn't want to tell me what, Dad?" I already knew the answer I sought. I knew it the moment I saw Mom in the kitchen. I didn't want to believe it. I wanted him to tell me.

"You know, things have been a little tough lately," Dad said, "you have heard Mom and me talk about it at dinner a few times. It's not like we wanted to hide anything from you; we didn't want to say anything until we found out." He stood from the trailer and walked over to the lawn, where an armchair awaited his attention. He lifted it easily with both hands. I watched him closely, knowing what he was going to say. He moved to push the armchair into the back of the trailer alongside the sofa. I waited him out. He sweated. I waited just shy of the panic attack lurking inside of me. He turned to face me again. "Well, I quit my job, Ali." It was my turn to lean against the trailer. "It wasn't working out the way I wanted it to. They promised me more funds. They promised me a better position." Out came the handkerchief again to swipe across his tired face. I hadn't noticed

26

until that moment how wrinkled his face had become. When did that happen? "It's been five years, Ali. I gave them five years, and they have not given what they promised. We can't make it here anymore, son." He tugged at the damp tee shirt clinging to his chest and arms. "It's time to go home."

"This is our home," I said.

"You know what I mean, Alister." Dad stared at me as if he were too tired to fight with words. "I have accepted a job back at my old employer in England. You will be able to catch up with your old friends there. You will be fine." He reached up to ruffle my hair as he did when I was a kid, and I ducked his reach.

"I was seven, Dad. Those weren't my friends. They were kids I went to primary school with. I was only in year two. I don't know those people anymore."

My Dad rubbed my arm and patted it gently. "It'll be alright, mate. I promise." He went back to lifting furniture from the lawn.

"What are you doing with this furniture?" I called after him.

"We're going to take it to your Mom's Aunt Edna," he answered. "She has a place to store it. In case we might need it again. I told her she could use it, but she said it would be fine in her garage for a while. Just in case."

"In case what?" I didn't know what he was saying. "In case we come back?"

Dad stopped with a table half off the trailer and looked at me, "Now, Alistair, you know the answer to that. We aren't going to come back. Once was enough. We tried it. Nan and Granddad are happy we are coming home. Enough said, then, yes? Once I get this trailer loaded we are off to Aunt Edna's."

"I have to go tell Tommy and Frankie," I wasn't sure what I would tell them.

"Run and tell them, then get right back. We must clear the house today and sleep at the airport hotel tonight. We leave first thing in the morning."

"Wow, you really did wait to tell me at the last minute." It wasn't fair. I didn't want to go. My life was here. My friends were here. I took off before he could answer back. I jumped on my bike and raced out of the driveway.

We met as arranged and hugged all around. No tears were spilled, but Frankie's welled up a bit. They headed back to watch TV at Tommy's, and I returned to help my parents pack up the house. We went to England, but my friends and the Poland Hill house never left my dreams.

Mrs. Wintergreen was still speaking, and my attention was directed back to her. "Well, I'm glad you can see the beauty here, Mr. Prescott." She rubbed her hand against her dress as if ridding it of soil. That was very odd. Maybe she had a nervous habit of a sort. "I will

28

leave you to your new home. I have another appointment at 2:00 this afternoon." She turned and tiptoed across the floor, which I supposed was to keep from slipping on the polished marble, and returned to the towering front doors. I followed behind her as she spoke. "Good day, Sir." She said as she used her entire body motion to open the left door and turned to face me. "Don't hesitate to contact me should you need anything else from me." She glanced around the inside of the lobby. "Let me know if you need any referrals for any contract work you might need to have done. They should be more likely to help if you call them directly." She smiled widely at me with her mouth, but the smile did not reach her eyes.

I lifted her hand and brought it to my lips. "Of course. Thank you again, Madam, for making all the purchase arrangements for me and my attorney. It doesn't look like I will be needing any assistance at this time. And I do have my friend, Tom Smith, arriving sometime today if my understanding is correct. If I find anything that requires repair, I am sure he will assist me."

Mrs. Wintergreen smiled, though her expression was one of confusion, yet she nodded her understanding. "I am sure he will, Mr. Prescott. Goodbye now."

She went through the door, and I watched to ensure she reached the bottom of the concrete steps before I shut the door and returned to the lobby.

The House on Poland Hill

In my wildest dreams, I would not have imagined this day a reality. I had purchased the Poland Hill Mansion. What an incredible luxury. I worked very hard as a Barrister most of my adult life and socked away a great deal of wealth. Certainly more than I would have ever needed to live quietly for the rest of my life in my cottage in rural England. But I didn't intend to live quietly. I intended to purchase this incredible property and reopen it to the masses. After the purchase was completed, I had expected to add a great deal of funds to the refurbishment of the establishment. What good fortune to find the work already finished. All I could imagine was that the investment company that owned the property had it refurbished prior to placing it on the market. What good fortune I now found myself in with the repairs completed. Having kept in touch with Tom and Frank for all these many years, Tom did not hesitate to act as my attorney-in-fact to sign the appropriate purchase agreement documents to get the ball rolling.

I glanced at the gilded lobby, and I could not contain a childhood giggle as my hands grabbed the ascot hanging around my neck. Where on earth should I start? I realized I had absent-mindedly twisted the scarf. I couldn't wait to see what all the rooms in the hotel had to offer, but the tower spire called to me first. I spun on my heels and scanned every wall of the lobby. The south wall contained the front entrance with the extravagant towering mahogany and brass doors. The west wall held open rooms that could be spaces for a restaurant, public house, and health spa, to be sure. I anticipated excitedly confirming what exactly they contained. Grand staircases rose against the north and east walls, covered in deep, rich burgundy carpeting to keep people from slipping on the smooth gray marble, hence finding themselves at the bottom in a heap. I laughed again at the sheer ornate beauty and majesty of the place. King Charles of England would feel at ease in this space. But I could not locate any place which appeared to be a gateway to the tower.

I raced over to fling open the colossal mahogany doors and hurried down the outside front steps. I ran past my Roadster, which stood still, waiting near the bottom of the steps and partly into the south yard. Funny, I didn't remember parking on the lawn. Curious. I turned and gazed above me. There it was, the same tower spire that filled my dreams, both at night and in my waking hours. I felt warm from excitement, tugged the ascot from my neck, and tossed it into my open convertible auto—bloody fool to have worn it today with this fine weather anyway.

I laughed and jaunted back up the concrete steps and into the foyer. The tower had given up its hiding place. I raced to the north staircase and bounded up the steps like I was that twelve-year-old boy, not the middle-aged man I had somehow become. I reached the second floor in mere moments. And there was, against the southern wall, a room gaping open to the hallway, a staircase rising within—the tower. How could I not see this entrance from the lobby floor? There was no way it could have been hidden from my sight from below. How did I not notice this entrance on the floor plans I reviewed years ago? Had I forgotten the tower started on the second floor?

There was no door to close off the tower entrance from any hotel guests. Only a beautiful gold chain stretched from wall to wall with a hanging sign. "No Admittance. Hotel Employees Only." How odd. One would think someone in their cups could stoop under the chain and take the circular staircase up to their demise. Why had the hotel left it this way? There had been many, many deaths reported during the hotel's existence, yet I had not heard of anyone taking a plunge from the tower. I would have believed they would have replaced the golden chain with something more secure. A locked door, perhaps— something to ponder upon.

I stooped low and stepped under the chain and into the room. It was dark within. My eyes followed the circular iron staircase reflected in the hallway's light, up as far as I could, and saw a hint of sunlight coming through each leaded window embedded in the tower as it rose to the spire. I pulled my mobile phone from my front trouser pocket and walked to the room entryway. I shone the mobile flashlight across the wall in search of a light switch and found one. It looked like the original knob and tube wiring installed in the original construction of the hotel. Of course, it was. And it looked pristine. I didn't see a speck of rust on the turn knob. I twisted the knob to the right. The glowing light revealed lighting sconces on the wall rising to the very top of the spire. What good fortune they were in working condition.

Glory be, I wouldn't need to use my mobile phone torch and risk missing one of the narrow iron steps rising steeply above me. I giggled with childish joy and raced to the bottom of the first riser. I couldn't remember laughing so much since my youth as I had today. I slipped my mobile back into my front pants pocket and ascended. I had assumed there would be a number of platform floors along the way, maybe not on every floor. The hotel had five floors: the lobby floor, three for guest rooms, and a fifth that gave rise to the domed ceiling. However, the tower loomed several stories higher. There should be at least three or four platforms in the tower itself. There was no way any workman could climb the entire height and not need a small rest along the way. I was correct. Peering to the top of the spire, I could detect four—the exact number as the windows I had viewed from the driveway. I reached the first such platform at about a five-story height. I stepped through the gap in the staircase's handrail and gently toed the platform at my feet.

After so many years of neglect, I wanted to be sure it would hold my weight. Of course, it did. It probably felt as sturdy as the day they built it. I moved the other foot onto it and did a little hop up and down just to be sure. Pristine, like the rest of the hotel. The wall sconce at this level reflected the light against what appeared to be rows and rows of unused folding chairs waiting for the next party or wedding outside on the massive south-front lawn. Why would they keep them up this high? How did they carry them up all these steps, I wondered? Nevertheless, there were a great many if I should need them in the future. I walked around them, past the back of the staircase, to look out a leaded window that looked to the south and could see the blurred vision of my parked car in the drive.

I reflected on espying the spire from the outside and recollected four large rectangular windows rising on the front of the spire wall. If the first window appeared at this level, at a height of five floors, how tall must it make the spire? No wonder one could see it rising over treetops from the town below. It is a magnificent structure. As I stared through the window, the abstract design of the lead glass made the lawn quiver like the ocean. Well, no one said leaded glass was the right thing to use, did they?

I returned to the iron staircase to continue my journey up and noticed another smaller window facing north between the rows of chairs. I decided I must look through it to see what sights it held. I brushed the light brown curl from my face as I shuffled between the rows of chairs to keep from tipping them over and leaned in at shoulder level to peer through. A view of the lobby center was below me. After I descended, I would have to look near the rooms on the fifth floor to see if I could see this window. I certainly hadn't seen it from the lobby floor. Wait just a minute, I thought as I stood back up straight. The platform was five stories high in the stairwell, but the staircase had started on the second floor above the lobby. If the stairs began on the second floor, and this platform was five stories high, then the window should look out on what would have to be the sixth floor above the lobby. However, there was no sixth floor. I should be looking at the middle of the dome. If one looked up from the lobby floor, only four floors rose above it. Not six. The fifth-floor walls ascended to aid the pillars with the support of the domed ceiling. Suppose the window looked out onto the fifth-floor hallway. It would mean the window had to be on the fourth floor, not the fifth, inside the tower. I was baffled but too eager to continue with this line of thought. It made no sense.

The following two platforms, placed only two floors above the prior, held no secrets or overstocked furniture. They were bare except for a small milking stool on each. I supposed they were spots to rest if needed during the climb.

I did not stop to rest and looked up to gauge the distance of the next platform. It appeared to be at least five or six floors higher. I took a deep breath, shook each leg, and continued upward until I was there, at the top platform in the spire. The platform, which gave rise to the top of the spire pyramid, was a glory to see. It was divided into three small rooms. The largest included the front window facing the south lawn and a large gabled window on the north side of the wall. I hurried over to look out and could see over the top of the domed roof to the north yard on the other side of the manor. In the distance, across a large expanse of grass, I could see the descending curve of the hill. And there, rising over the tops of the lower trees, I glimpsed the top of a Ferris wheel beyond. Oh, I had known the property contained an old amusement park. But how fortunate I was to witness it on my first day here. I turned from the view and took in my surroundings.

Someone had adorned the room with a comfortable and amply quilted bed, an overstuffed chair with a footstool at the ready, and a side table situated precisely where it needed to be between the bed and the chair. A tall floor lamp with a jeweled Tiffany Favrile glass globe shimmered with an iridescence to light the entire room. Fabulous. I could picture one here, with a book in hand, whiling away the hours until morning. One could see the whole of the south lawn and drive leading to the hotel and the north lawn overlooking the amusement park facilities. How glorious a space in which to spend time. I decided right then this was where I would spend my first night. The bed was ready to crawl into. I turned to inspect the other two smaller rooms: a wash closet with a lavatory and a small kitchen. How ingenious. I assumed this was where the caretaker must have resided, the hotel staff and guests carrying on below, without knowing he could see almost everything from the windows in this room. Fascinating. Why would he want to spy on everyone from this elevation? Wouldn't it have been simpler to meander through the hotel grounds? I could not see the hot health spas from here nor the hot springs that fed them, though I could glimpse a sign advertising them beside the gravel road leading through the trees and down the hill to the amusement park. I noticed a large tool shed near the southwest corner of the mansion. A handy place to keep awnings, tables, and such for any outdoor events.

I turned my head to return to the stairway when a dark shadow stepped between me and the window. I jumped back a foot, overwhelmed with astonishment, and to remove myself from its path. The rising hair on the nape of my neck and arms sent an electric current of horror up my spine. I couldn't move. Loosely shaped like a large man, I watched, aghast, as the shadow leaned over to peer through the glass window where I had just been standing. I flushed in fear.

Great Scott! I had heard this house, hotel, and property on the top of Poland Hill were haunted all my life. But, I was a man of intelligence and curiosity, and while I had always believed it was true, I really hadn't expected to see them myself. Had I? Of course, I bought the property, didn't I? This would lead you to think I was sure I would be able to see them. I had been inside the hotel for less than a day, and this shadow, this ghost, appeared before me. I stood paralyzed and watched it with both horror and wonder.

It seemed forever, but the ghost finally moved away from the window and walked through the wall into the lavatory. I wiped the sweat from my brow and hurried to chase it into the other room. It was gone. Despite my fear, I chuckled and lowered myself onto the floor beside the stairway handrail. The chuckle reverberated through my body, and a solitary sob escaped my lips. I grabbed the handrail to lift myself to my feet but was not rewarded. Great wracking sobs spilled from my mouth, surprising my ears, and I sat back on the floor.

I should not have left my ascot in the auto. It would have been helpful as I had no neckerchief or handkerchief to mop my face and brow. Tears fell unfettered to my lap. I listened as my sobs gave way again to laughter. One might have thought I had gone quite mad sitting on the tower spire platform.

The light began to wane. I roused myself from the stupor in which I had fallen and realized it was starting to get dark. The sun no longer brightened the space. Shadows began to creep in. I had no realization of how long I sat on the floor, but I knew I had no intention of spending the night in this little bedroom any longer. Grabbing the

Kathryn Cain

handrail, I pulled myself to my feet and stepped down onto the iron step below me. I took no time to stop and rest on the other platforms. My wobbly legs descended as quickly as I could.

I reached the bottom in no time and rushed from the tower entry through the hall to the grand staircase and down into the lobby. The first chair I came to rested against one of the marble pillars, and I slid into it quickly to still my wobbling legs. After wrapping my arms around the pillar, I felt the marble's cooling effect on my chest and arms through my jacket. I lay my face against the extraordinary smoothness of the marble and went to sleep.

Chapter Three

My ears brought sounds of wailing into my sleeping brain. I peeked open my eyes, my face still pressed against the cool marble of the pillar, and squinted toward the direction of the unsettling sound. What unearthly noise affronted me? I had forgotten where I was, and reality hit me like a brick. I was inside the house on Poland Hill. The sun was gone, and I was glad I had left the lobby lamps on. I lifted my face from the pillar and moved my head in the same direction as my eyes. The wailing was coming from the direction of the east staircase. I sat up, turned in that direction, and leaped to my feet. An apparition appeared right before my eyes.

A female apparition wafted from thin air and then manifested into an almost solid being. Almost. I could still see the wall lights through its form. The ghost, spirit, whatever it was, emitted a funereal keening that unnerved me. I stood rooted to the floor in a mixture of startlement, shock, and numbness. She knelt on the floor before a small rocking cradle filled with white linens and laced quilts. She had been a woman of means. Her wailing stopped abruptly, and she looked up at me, tears spilling out of her blackened eyes and down her pale, sunken cheeks. She rose slowly to her feet, her long, ragged skirts bound around her ankles, and she tripped back a step. I never thought a ghost could trip. She didn't take her eyes from mine as she lifted a slender, bony arm and pointed down into the crib. She blubbered once, and the wailing began anew.

I was spellbound. I didn't know what to do. My legs locked in paralyzation, but the apparition would not release my gaze as it continued to point into the slowly rocking crib. It wanted me to look into the crib. Fingers of fear crept up my spine and locked onto the back of my neck. Who was this woman? A bonnet covered her head of long, thin, gray hair that tumbled to her waist. Her garb was as if she lived or died in the seventeen hundreds. The hotel had not been in existence at that time. How had she come to be here? Her wailing grew louder, her finger ever pointing. With a sudden sense of sorrow, I was jolted from my horror and moved toward her.

She again knelt beside the crib as I approached and drew back the quilt as I dropped to a knee and peered in. I stared at the child's eyes, locked open, sightless, and quite dead. Half of the child's facial skin, no, not the skin, half of the child's face was missing, the skull bone ragged. What had happened to this infant? The woman's wailing stopped, and she began mewling, her eyes upturned to me in pleading. The child's remaining skin was mottled and dark with lividity. The specter reached in and plucked the child from the crib and held it to her breast. She kissed its misshapen head, then held the child out to me. I didn't know what she wanted me to do. I couldn't take it from her. Even if I could, my revulsion wouldn't allow me. Sorrow for her overwhelmed me, and I sat down on the floor.

"I can't," I whispered. "I don't know what you want me to do. I can't help your baby." I ran a hand over the side of the crib, and it passed right through the rails. "I can't help you, Madam. I am sorry." Tears sprang to my own eyes as she brought the child back to her breast, held it close, and began rocking. She kissed its head, gave one more sob and pleading stare, and then, they faded from my sight.

Just like that, they were gone.

I wiped the tears from my cheeks and surveyed my surroundings.

"Well," I said aloud, "that was interesting."

I rose from the floor and brushed the back of my pants offhandedly. However, no dust fell from them. I returned to the chair I had slept on and picked up my mobile phone from where it had fallen on the seat. It was only 10:00 p.m. I had not been here an entire night yet had witnessed two visitations. Two different specters.

I had the sudden urge to call Tom and Frankie. After all, I had to tell them the news. I have witnessed the truth of the old stories. I first tried to reach Tommy and then Frankie. I reached only their voicemails. I left messages on each.

"You are not going to believe this. It's true, Tom, it's all true. The stories, I mean." He was going to think I was as scatterbrained as my staccato message, but I plunged on excitedly. "It is haunted, Tommy. I

42

purchased it just this morning, as you know, and I met Mrs. Wintergreen here at about noon today. And it's beautiful, just like we knew it would be. And I've already seen two ghosts. Well, three, really, but one was dead. I mean, really dead. Not like the other two who were, well, ghosts." I sounded like that twelve-year-old boy to my own ears. I couldn't imagine how I sounded to Tommy. "Call me right away," I continued, "it doesn't matter the time. Call as soon as you get this." I clicked off.

"Frank," I said into the phone, "this is Alister, I'm here, I mean, you know where I am, and we were right. It is haunted. Call me back right away."

I spun around to ensure I was alone in the lobby. I was. There was no way I was going to be able to sleep tonight. Should I stay here? Should I go back to the hotel where I stayed last night?

After leaving the messages for Tom and Frank, I knew they would think I should stay. I should look through every room tonight if I could. I was too frightened and yet too alive. I felt utterly alive. Electricity surged through my body and limbs. I knew I couldn't leave yet. I looked at the silent phone and bounced it in my palm. I had to keep this with me. Would the ghosts have shown up on my phone if I had taken a picture? The one in the tower was only a shadow, but the lady, the mother with her baby, could have shown up; indeed, she would have. Could it have been captured in a photograph? I just knew

43

she would have. I had to try. Would I see any more tonight? My thoughts tripped without the benefit of lucidity through my brain, and I knew it was early yet.

After slipping the phone into my left front pants pocket, I jogged to the front of the lobby near the colossal south doors. With my back to the front desk, I surveyed my surroundings. I could see all four floors above me. Except for the tower entrance, the hotel guest's rooms adorned the second and third-floor hallways. The fourth and fifth floors had more oversized doors the size of gathering places and party rooms, perhaps. There was a row of door knobs around the top wall, just below where the dome began to rise away. The knobs were attached to what looked like deep drawers, which one could pull open to store items. How odd. One would have to use a ladder to reach the drawers, and they ran around the entire walls of the fifth floor. I wondered what on earth they would store in those.

Then I saw it, on the fourth floor, the window that looked in from the tower platform. Interesting, indeed. I could not wrap my intellect around it being there, two stories below the window inside the tower. Later, I found many things about the hotel I could not explain.

Two large glass doors stood open into a room almost wholly hidden behind the north staircase directly across the lobby from me. I would start there. After that, I would inspect every room from the first floor to the fifth.

I pulled out my mobile to check the battery level. It was full. I slid it back into the pocket whence it came and moved across the lobby at a trot. I passed the pillar with the chair where I had dozed and moved behind the sprawling risers of the north stairs. Entering through the parted glass of the doors, I saw the dining room. I had assumed the restaurant was one of the lobby's west wall doors. But it was here, hidden behind the north staircase. White linen and utensil-covered tables filled the space. Sparkling glasses waited to be filled with fresh, cool water, and napkins sat ready to be placed on diners' laps. I could almost hear the sounds of chatter, food preparation, and banging of dishes coming from the kitchen. I was sure I caught a trace of seared beef wafting through the air. Fascinating.

I moved past the tables and entered the kitchen. The aromas of baking pies and loaves of bread made my mouth water. Somewhere in my brain, I noted I had neither lunch nor dinner today. I hurried past the large ovens and felt warmth as I headed out a side door that led to a hallway. The hall moved away from the kitchen toward the back of the hotel.

I had studied the house's architectural plans years ago. I was sure the layout was ingrained in me still. Yet, I had no recollection of this hallway leading from the kitchen. Of course, I didn't remember the tower began at the second-floor level either. I shook my head to clear my thoughts and return to the task before me. Where did the hallway lead?

My phone beeped. I had a voicemail. I hadn't even heard it ring. I hit the icon for the message, and Tommy's voice rang loudly and clearly.

"Hey, Alister, my man." I could hear glasses clinking behind his raised voice. "Sorry, I missed your call. Lisa and I are at a wedding party. It looks like it is going to go until midnight. I will call you in the morning, buddy." Voices laughed behind him.

They were at a wedding. It was a Friday night. My thoughts drifted away. I was married once. I was in my late twenties. Her name was Agnes, and I loved her more than life. Full of spirit and laughter, her smile brought joy to my eyes and warmed my heart. We met with several couples on a regular weekly basis. It was usually dinner at each other's homes. We had beautiful conversations and camaraderie. Sometimes, we met at a local pub in the neighborhood where we all lived. Often, I shared the rumored stories of ghosts and my desire to purchase the house on Poland Hill. At first, they were intrigued. But they began to change. After a few short years, our chums started canceling our dinner engagements. They feigned sicknesses, working late at the office, issues with parents or children—that kind of thing. Then Agnes became cold and hurtful. She began to belittle me at every turn. My wife and mates had gone from

46

being excited with me to not believing in me. Because they had not seen what I had seen, they could not and chose not to believe in what I knew to be true.

That black, wrought iron fence had told me the truth. I had touched it and seen its truth. Frank and Tom had touched it but had not felt a thing. Yet, they had believed me. They believe me still. Agnes left me without so much as a note to say goodbye. Just a gaping empty closet remained. I believed in her, but she did not believe in me. Sometimes, I miss her terribly. But then I think of the hidden whispers between her and our mates and remember.

It was not long after that I lost my parents. They died quite young, and after they followed Granddad and Nan to the Great Beyond, I never spoke of the house on Poland Hill again. I had soured on relationships, except with Tom and Frankie. I found the opportunity to retire from my post and make the move I had dreamed of since childhood. Returning to Prophet, South Carolina, where my best chums Tom and Frank lived, felt good. They were the only two who ever understood and still believed in me.

I suddenly heard speaking in my ear and returned my attention to the mobile. Tom was saying, "I couldn't hear your message, man. There was a lot of static. I didn't hear anything, actually, but I recognized your number." There was a lot of noise in the background. "I gotta go, man. I hope everything went okay today. I can't wait for you to invite me to see it. We have been waiting years, man. You will have enough room for Lisa, me, and the kids to come." Lisa told him to get off the phone. They were going to raise another toast. "I miss you, man. I'm glad you finally came home. Talk to you tomorrow. Chin Chin!" Then he was gone.

"Chin Chin," I said to the silent phone. I talked to Tom almost weekly. He knew I was signing on the house this morning. Did he tell me he wouldn't be around today? Why can't I remember? I looked at the phone. The battery was half gone. How did that happen? I had just looked at it, and it was fully charged.

I looked at the hall stretching before me—no time like the present. I started down the completely white-walled, white-floor tiled hall. How did they keep the white floor so clean? What an odd thought. Who did I think they were? The hall seemed to follow an arc, not a straight line. There were no windows or doors, only sconced lighting to break the solid line of the walls. I thought it might have been a hallway used to bring produce to the kitchen, but after five minutes of walking, the idea seemed unreasonable. After I had begun to think it led nowhere, it gradually started downhill. Just a bit, but enough to feel it. How odd. In a short time, the gradual slope became steeper and the hall walls closer. Maybe it led down through the hill to the amusement park. A secret entrance for employees, perhaps. As it held no windows, anything was possible. I hurried my step as excitement began to build within me. I was glad the flooring was dry, or I might have slipped or slid. I placed my hands flat on the wall to each side and tried to slow my footing. The hallway ended abruptly, and I arrived with a thump as my derriere landed on the ground a foot below, the hallway rising behind me.

"Oof. How brilliant. An almost vertical hallway." It is no wonder the hall hadn't been drawn on the blueprints. The prints didn't include any basement or below-ground room, precisely where I found myself—sitting on a lumpy concrete subfloor slab. The lighting from the white hall did little to shine brightness around this lower, darkened space.

After waiting a brief moment for the tingling of my spine to ease, I raised to my feet, pulled my mobile from my pocket, pleased to see it was undamaged, and turned the torch on. Nothing out of the ordinary exposed itself to the light. One expected to see a row of ladders, wheelbarrows, and a sundry of garden tools strewn about. Though there were also no windows in this relatively small workroom, a door led out directly across from the hallway tunnel from whence I came.

I moved a six-foot ladder out of my path, then raised my phone above my head to light the way. The door was wooden, and compared to the pristine care of the rest of the mansion, it was pitted, unvarnished, and worn. The doorknob was tarnished and did not turn. The darkness, the uneven concrete floor, and the filth inside the room made it feel as if I had entered an entirely different property.

"Down the rabbit hole, Alice," I laughed despite the current state of my heart as it beat wildly within my chest. I slid my phone between my lips and used both hands to grasp the doorknob. I twisted, turned, and pulled with all my strength to no avail.

"This is a turn of events," I mumbled around my phone, then pulled it from my lips. A workbench appeared to my left in a brief glimpse of passing light. I returned the light toward it, and there it was. A tinplate steel oil can. It was precisely what was needed to attempt to unstick the rusted doorknob. I took two steps toward the bench, and a deep chill brushed against my skin. The hair on my arms instantly stood up. I reached out my hand and grasped the container.

My hand was not the only one holding onto it. My heart, which had already been beating wildly, nearly lurched from my chest. I snatched my hand back and leaped two steps backward so quickly one might have thought I had gotten burnt. The specter lifted the oil can from the work table where I had abandoned it and held it aloft before him.

"Now, I need to use that," I stuttered. "I would like to unstick the door over there." I pointed behind me as if the ghost didn't know to which door I referred.

As I listened to my heart pounding within my ears, I realized my body also trembled. I have thought of this and the prior two ghostly moments all of my life. From the moment I heard the rumors of this haunted mansion in my youth, visions of running into a manifestation filled my head during the days and my dreams at night. I had become comfortable with thoughts of the truth of it, yet now my body trembled, and my thudding heart betrayed me as I attempted to control myself. Though the chill of fear crept through my body, I willed my shaking hand to steady the phone, hence the torch, and light the ghost before me. The light did not go through him as it had the mourning mother, and he cast a dark shadow on the wall behind.

"Great, Scott," I exclaimed. "What manner of ghost are you? Why, my light does not pass through you. You look as corporeal as I do." Despite the cold, a dribble of sweat escaped my scalp and slithered down my right cheek. I lifted my shoulder to smudge it off as I held the phone out in front of me. "Are you just going to be silent?" I egged it on. What was I doing?

The specter just stood there looking at me with the oil can held out in front of him. He looked like a jovial fellow. His rounded belly was snug within his suspendered pants, and an Irish tam tilted askew upon his brown-haired head. His bright blue eyes sparkled as he nodded to me and then to the can.

"You want me to take it?" I queried. "I would have had it if you had not gotten to it before I did." I shuffled two steps back in his direction. I believe he just wanted to be helpful and give it to me. I reached out and took it from him. The can was chilled and cold in my hand. "Well, thank you, Sir. I appreciate your assistance." I pulled the can into my chest to warm it, hoping the lubricant would run smoothly. Turning to approach the frozen lock of the door, I glanced over my shoulder to keep an eye on him. He had disappeared into the room's darkness with my light now trained upon the door.

"I say, old boy," I called over my shoulder as I tipped the oil can into the keyhole on the weathered door, "were you the gardener here, perchance?" I didn't expect him to answer me. However, I had heard the wailings of the sorrowed mother and thought it might be a possibility. I placed my phone precariously between my teeth again, dropped to one knee, and raised the can to sprinkle oil around the frozen doorknob while attempting to turn it to and fro. It didn't budge. I kept at it and added oil in the space between the lock and the striker plate on the jamb, hoping some would slide into the latch. After setting the oil can at my knee, I pulled the phone from my teeth and flashed it in his direction.

The smile surrounded by his chubby pink cheeks was unnervingly eerie.

"Egad!" I started in surprise and immediately thought of a horrific little leprechaun. His smile then split into a vast, grotesque grin. My eyes at once narrowed in on his Machiavellian grin. I was shocked to my core and plopped to the ground. His body inflated before my eyes and began to rise, bobbing like a balloon on a string, as he leered at me. Red bulging veins threatened to burst from his once sparkling blue eyes. I found this more than terrifying. Do ghosts have blood? My rattled mind asked itself. A copious amount of green, slimy drool escaped that gaping mouth. The little scary leprechaun had turned into a hellish clown. I couldn't move. He opened his mouth, and a thunderous cacophony filled the room. I covered my ears to dim the sound and tightened my eyes against the ghoul before me.

In an instant, the sound was gone. I dropped my hands from my ears and opened my eyes to darkness. Where was my phone? I realized I had thrown it down to cover my ears. I rose to my knees and feverishly searched the floor around me. I couldn't see anything. I couldn't see the creature anymore, and that deepened my fear.

Where was it? My right thumb struck the mobile, and I grabbed it with both hands as if my life depended on it. Maybe it did. I lept to my feet and shined the torch up at the ceiling where I last saw the monstrosity hovering above me. I spun around the room so quickly that I thought I would trip. It was gone. I didn't hesitate any too long lingering there. I fled back to the strange vertical hallway and lunged into it. Scrambling to right myself, I braced my hands and feet against the wall, hurled myself over the few vertical feet, and landed in the hallway. I raced up the sloping floor until it seemed level below my feet and slowed just enough to glance behind me, just in case. The wall sconces glowed brightly against the white-painted walls. I was alone. My chest heaved, my breath hot, and my lungs raw. I bent over at the waist and wanted to throw up. I did not. When I finally had my wits about me, I stood tall and sighed in relief. What a fool was I. I chuckled as I replayed my last few moments in my mind's eye. What a stunning display of courage. Hahaha!

I looked at my phone. It was only ten thirty. How could it be? It seemed hours since I had awoken on the chair in the lobby. Had the clock stopped working? Was it possible? I trudged the rest of the way back into the hotel kitchen. After opening three cabinets, I pulled a glass out and stopped at the sink. The water was cool and refreshing. Someone spent a lot of time ensuring everything here was in working order. I was grateful to them. After chugging down three glasses and splashing some water onto my face, I wiped my face with my sleeve, exited the dining room, and returned to the lobby.

I crossed the large expanse and locked the front door securely. Suddenly, I needed to ensure all the outside windows and doors were locked. I raced frantically around the lobby walls, opened, closed, and locked every window and door to be sure no one could get in. Sweat returned to my brow.

"Enough," I yelled out loud. The word echoed around the lobby. This childishness had to stop.

I willed myself to calm my breathing and set out looking for a linen closet. I found one on the second floor, beside the tower's entry room. I pulled out some sheets and a large cotton blanket. With my arms loaded with linens, I turned to go back down the staircase.

Curiosity then got the better of me, and I went into the tower room and looked up through the spiral staircase. I had left all the lights on. I walked to the knob and tube switch beside the doorway and shut them off. I went back to the center of the room and looked up again. The dark shadow I had seen on the first tower floor now appeared to glow radiant white as it circled lazily between the stairs and the walls. Circling and circling, calling me to come back up. I ignored it, returned to the first floor, and spread the sheets and blanket on a sofa. I'd had enough for one day.

Chapter Four

Saturday morning came before I was ready. My night had been filled with dark dreams of chaos. I sat up and looked around and remembered where I was. I had slept with all the lobby lights on.

I slipped my feet into my shoes, shook out my brown waves, ran my hands over them to smooth them down, and went in search of something to eat in the kitchen. I found a loo off the dining room and stopped for the morning's business.

The bouquet of freshly brewed coffee and baked pastries filled the kitchen. What good fortune. A pot of coffee sat on the stove, and a cup and a plate of pastries were on the counter beside it. I poured a cup and held it below my nose. The aroma was heavenly, and I took a sip. It was hot and marvelous. I set the cup down and picked up a raspberry tart. It was divine. Who put these here? Hadn't I locked up tight before I went to sleep?

Just then, I heard singing from the butler's pantry, and a woman about my age, I determined, emerged with her hands full of tins. She visibly jumped when she saw me.

"Oh, hello, Sir," she said. "Good morning to you." She set the tins on the metal table in the center of the kitchen. "I'm just getting some things together to prepare a nice lunch for you." She set about pulling pots from beneath the table on a hidden shelf.

"I'm sorry, Miss," I rattled off, "I wasn't aware anyone was here but me." I set the tart back on the plate and picked up the cup of coffee. "Do I have you to thank for such a wonderful breakfast?" I queried.

"Oh, it's nothing, Sir." She plunked a pot onto the gas stovetop and turned to me with her hand out for a shake. "I'm Molly." She said. "I take care of the kitchen here."

I held my cup in my left hand and gave her hand a polite shake. "Well, Molly, I am Alister Prescott. I just purchased this property this morning."

"Oh, I know who you are, Sir. We have all heard you were coming."

"I am so glad," I said. Who was we? "I'm afraid nobody told me about you." I picked up the coffee pot and poured more into my cup.

"I can't imagine why not," Molly responded. "I've been here forever, Sir." She moved to search in a drawer for something. "I am responsible for running the household. It's a pretty big job, but it keeps me busy." She pulled out a giant can opener. "I have sent the kitchen staff to task. We will have a glorious gala for you tomorrow night. We have already sent out the invitations. It will be a marvelous start to welcoming you home, Sir."

Her words were curious. Who are we, and how were they planning a party for me so quickly? I was quite pleasantly surprised. What fun. All thoughts of last night disappeared, and I was eager to hear the details of the party.

"Did Mrs. Wintergreen ask you to include Thomas Smith and Frank Franklin when sending the invitations?" I certainly hoped so, but they were just a phone call away.

"I'm afraid I don't know a Thomas Smith or Frank Franklin, Mr. Prescott. But we made sure all of your old friends were invited, so they must be on the list." She opened the can nearest her and dumped what looked like beans into a huge pot. I presumed you could precook beans the day before.

"I don't understand," I was perplexed. "How could you know of all of my old friends? I mean, I was twelve when I left town, and there were basically only Tommy and Frankie back then," I said, slipping into their comfortable, old names. "Other classmates, I suppose, ones whose names I can't remember now." I set my coffee cup on the center kitchen table and pulled out a chair to sit down and watch her work for a while. I had so many questions. Had she ever seen any of the ghosts I had?

I studied her attire and tried to place it. I was unfamiliar with household maids' clothing, but I thought it would have looked more modern. It was a typical pink uniform dress with the classic little white ruffled pink apron often seen in diners nationwide in the seventies.

"The entire town, Sir."

Molly was talking, and I pulled my head out of my thoughts to catch the end of what she said.

"I'm sorry, Molly. What about the entire town?" I asked.

"The welcome home party, Sir. The guests you asked about. We have invited the entire town." She turned the heat down on the beans and gave them a stir, her back to me. "Everyone has been very eager to see you again, Sir. They have been excited since they heard you were coming back to town."

"Why should the entire town be glad of my return?" I was incredulous. "I was only twelve years old when we moved back to London." I rose from my seat and walked over to the stove where she stood.

"You may have only been twelve, Sir," she continued, "but everyone knew you believed in them. And you did believe in them. Not many did." She wiped her hands on her apron and turned to face me. "They have been very eager for your return, to be able to talk with you."

"What do you mean, I believed in them, Molly? I was twelve. I barely knew anyone in town."

"Well, they knew you, Sir." And with that, she turned back to her duties.

"Well, I should think a great many of them are old now. Don't you think?" I picked up my coffee cup from the table and placed it in the sink. "I don't know what they would want to talk to me about," I muttered as I excused myself and left Molly to attend to her duties in the kitchen. What did they think I believed about them, I wondered. Oh well, I'm off to begin my inspection of each of the rooms. There had to be something inside this building that needed attending to.

Since I was still on the lobby floor, I decided to continue my search on the ground level. I walked the short distance to the west side of the lobby and entered through the first glass door. Etched upon it in gray lettering were the words Beauty Shop. I peeked around the sunlit room and saw nothing that piqued my interest. Two barber chairs were in front of two sinks. The only other thing in the room was a small waiting area. I could picture men and women from the nineteen twenties waiting for their turn in the chairs. I wondered what to do with this space and moved on to the next door. There were no etchings on the next door, and it was dark within. I opened the door and felt for the light switch. I found it with ease and turned it on.

The room was cavernous. It belied the smooth line of the outside wall of the mansion. It was a pub. The room's right side was just shy of being entirely made up of one long wooden bar counter. Large TV screens filled the wall on the left side of the room. Tables, each holding a tiny, dim lamp, with chairs filled the center of the room. What was this, I wondered?

I stepped across the threshold and stopped dead in my tracks. People instantly appeared and jamb-packed the dark, cavernous room. Dozens of people rose from their table seats simultaneously, screaming at the TV screens as horses raced across them in live action. Smoke filled the air as chubby men with fat cigars waived fists of money at the screens. Women in finery, holding martini glasses aloft, with fur wraps swinging, yelled at the screens along with their husbands. Cigarette girls walked between the tables as their trays hung from their necks while shouting, "Cigarettes, cigars."

I could hardly take it all in. I stepped a few steps into the room while I waived smoke from in front of my face. Wisps of it moved before me as I approached a man attending the long bar. Bottles of spirits lined the mirrored wall behind him.

"I say, Sir," I raised a hand to get his attention. "I say, Sir, what is going on here?" I asked him a pretty stupid question. I could see what was going on here.

Folks were betting on horse races in a room in the building I had just purchased yesterday. Another thing Mrs. Wintergreen had neglected to tell me. This building was currently in use. When had all the people arrived? They couldn't have all flocked here while I was in the kitchen this morning with Molly.

In conversation with a client, the man turned his attention toward me and smiled. He walked right over as he mopped the counter along the way. "Well, good morning, Mr. Prescott. Welcome to the Prancing Pony. What will you have?"

I was taken aback. "How do you know my name, Sir?" I asked.

"Aren't you the gentleman, Mr. Prescott, who purchased this fine establishment yesterday?"

"Why, yes, I am." What an idiot I am. Of course, he would know who I am. I stuck my hand out to him for a shake, and he took it with a smile.

"What will you have, Sir?" He asked again.

Was it afternoon, I thought? "I'll have a scotch on the rocks, please," I answered him, not really caring if it were afternoon.

"Coming right up, Sir." He turned away from me.

I took a seat at the bar and turned my attention toward the people at the tables and those pressed up against the long bar top. They dressed as if they lived when the hotel opened in the nineteen-twenties rather than in today's attire. I watched them yell, scream, and then cheer at the giant screens on the wall. I was born in the UK, and I have always been a studious fellow. I knew the first television was demonstrated by a Scottish lad, John Logie Baird, on March 25, 1925. It was called the Baird Televisor. Only about one thousand were sold to the public from 1930 to 1933. None made it to the United States. The screens looked like plasma flat-screen televisions, which didn't come out until Fujitsu created them in 1997. How could this be? The building has been vacant since the sixties. Even if flat screens had been available in the twenties, CBS aired the first horse race on television for the Belmont Stakes in 1948. It didn't add up. But I guess nothing added up in this establishment so far.

I looked down at the bar's opposite end and glimpsed a massive table laden with an array of meats, cheeses, and a large assortment of bread. Why hadn't Molly said anything about this? Maybe the beans she was working on were for in here, not for my welcome home party tomorrow night. Had she said it, and I didn't hear it?

The bartender returned with my scotch. "Here you are, Mr. Prescott."

"Thank you, Mr.., Mr."

"Reese, Sir. Charles Reese."

"Thank you, Mr. Reese." I accepted the glass from his hand and took a sip. He turned to go, and I said, "I wonder why Mrs. Wintergreen didn't tell me before my purchase yesterday that there was an active public house in the hotel."

He stopped and turned back to me. "I'm afraid I don't know a Mrs. Wintergreen, Sir." He mopped the bar top with a towel, where I slopped a bit of the drink from my glass at his answer.

"Tell me, Mr. Reese," I wasn't sure what I wanted to ask, "how long have you been working here?" I would start there.

"Oh," he glanced up as if the answer would fall from the ceiling, "it is going on five years now, Sir."

"Five years, how wonderful." I took another sip, and it trickled down my throat with a pleasant burn. "Let me ask you, Mr. Reese, exactly what year did you start working here?" I eyed him over the rim of my glass as I took another sip.

"Well, now, that would have been 1929, Sir."

I set my glass down firmly on the bar. A chunk of ice jumped out. "1929?"

"Yes, Sir. I started the year after the hotel opened."

"So, that would make this 1934. Is that correct, Mr. Reese?"

"Why, yes, of course, Mr. Prescott. I helped in the soup kitchen that the hotel ran from 1929 to 1933, then moved here this year to run the tavern when the hotel was allowed to open it."

I was beginning to understand. "1934. That would be after prohibition was over." I took another slug of my drink. " And when, then, did I come to buy the hotel, Mr. Reese?"

"Why, you know, Sir." He leaned in toward me and looked me straight in the eye. "You know you purchased it yesterday. You just said so, Sir. What is this all about?"

"Tell me then, Mr. Reese, if it is 1934, why are your patrons watching a horse race on a television that had not been invented until 1997?" I had him, I was sure.

"I don't know what you are rambling about, Mr. Prescott. The establishment's patrons are watching the horse race through that large window, right there in the wall," he pointed past my face, behind me.

Sweat broke upon my brow. I was afraid to turn and look. But I did. He was right. There were no wide flat-screen televisions on the wall, only one long glass window. The patrons no longer sat at their tables but stood at the window watching from as close as they could get. They jumped up and down, sloshed their drinks upon each other, and screamed the names of the horses they had bet upon.

"Are you feeling well, Sir?" Charles asked.

I had to come to grips with the fact that in this room, it was 1934. I had hoped Mr. Reese was disillusioned. The wide screens proved we were in the present. But we were not. They were ghosts. Every one of them. Suddenly, I remembered the fire. The fire which had consumed the hotel had started in this very room. The wooden bar seemed to move beneath my arms, and I tightened my grip on my glass. From the corner of my eye, I witnessed a bright yellow and red flame lick the countertop beside me. I felt heat upon my face. I lifted the glass to slam back the last sip of scotch, but it was empty. The glass exploded in my grasp.

I looked up in shock as glass shards rained down onto the burning bar. I panicked and scanned the room for Charles. He was gone. I looked around the now-empty room. They were all gone. Flames began to crawl up the walls around me. I slid off the barstool, my legs wobbling as they touched the ground. I ran to the lobby door from which I had entered and stepped out into the light. I spun around and looked behind me. The room was dark. I turned again and looked at the brightened lobby to get my bearings and calm my shaking. The tang of cigar smoke and char clung to my hair.

Chapter Five

The twin mahogany doors, still locked from last night, flung open as I ran outside. My car still sat where I parked it at noon yesterday. I ran past it and around the southeast corner of the mansion. The yard was several acres in size but was all grass. There was no race track. Any hint one had existed had long since disappeared.

I returned to the driveway, scratching my head with confusion. Somehow, I realized I had not changed my clothes this morning after having slept in them and been wearing them since yesterday. I could detect a slight musty odor from sweat that was not pleasing to the nose. I went to my auto, found the keys still in my pants pocket, and retrieved my satchel from the boot. I briefly thought about the weather and looked up into the sky. My experience is that the sun was reaching high noon. How could that be? Boy, time seems to stand still around here. I had accomplished so much this morning by meeting and spending time with Molly in the kitchen and having a cocktail in the public house.

I digress, back to the weather. I had been on Poland Hill Road that day and had seen it rain at the top of the hill while the sun was high in the sky below in town. I decided I would take the precaution of impending rain and raise the roof of my Roadster. I slipped into the vehicle and did just that. I exited, grabbed my satchel from the gravel where I had set it, and looked up at the mansion. A shiver slid up my spine. What an accomplishment I had made. I could not believe it was mine. I had dreamed of this moment all my life and found it hard to believe it was true. The spire windows twinkled as if they winked at me from above. Almost as if the house itself knew I was finally here.

I suddenly perceived the air felt thicker up here, not from the slight elevation, but something more sinister. I had not felt this yesterday, but it was suddenly very apparent. The front doors had been left open in my haste and appeared as a vast, dark maw awaiting my return. The fear I felt last night returned like a hard slap to my face. Sitting in that pub, talking to Charles Reese, and having that scotch had been a brief release. Until the fire, it was an oddity at best. I knew it would happen, the ghosts. It was the real heat of the Pub fire that had me shaking. But last night, that had been different.

It was the monstrous entity in the basement, lurking in front of that worn, old door. I had to go back there. I had to see what was behind that door.

Perspiration trickled down the nape of my neck, and it registered in my mind that I still stood there looking at those massive gaping doors. I moved up the concrete steps hesitantly and passed through them. I closed them firmly behind me but intentionally left them unlocked, just in case.

The first step, I determined, was to find a room to call my own, clean up, and don new clothes. I jaunted up the west staircase to the second floor and went around the southside hallway. I stopped at the entryway to the spire. The top floor of the spire was clean. Someone had dressed the bed in plush quilts, so it was move-in ready. I wondered if Molly had taken care of that. It had its bathroom close at hand. I walked to the foot of the stairs and looked up. It was dark, save for the sunlight floating in those leaded windows, and I could not see the top floor platform. What was I thinking? Why would I want to climb those stairs every day and night? And, I thought, why would Molly choose that high room to have ready? It didn't make any sense. I hurried into the hallway and decided on the first guest room to the east.

Guest Suite Room 108. I turned the knob, and the white door swung open with ease. I peeked inside. It was bright and clean. It was a drawing room. No bed was in sight, but I saw no spider webs or dust. Molly's crew must take care of the entire place. Thank you, Molly. I crossed the threshold, and the lighting seemed to shift slightly. I dropped my satchel where I stood and took a couple more steps into the room.

The whirring sound of an old film projector filled the room. It sat on a dresser to my right. The film ran on the sprockets from the supply reel through the projector, but rather than winding onto the takeup reel, it puddled down onto the floor like an ever-growing wreath of snakes, boiling over and over each other. I moved closer to see what movie was projected onto the adjacent wall. The spewing light brightened the dust particles swirling in the air, giving the area a movie theater vibe. It was not lost on me that the movie showed this room. However, in the film, I was not standing in the center of the room as I found myself now. The film showed a door opening from my left, and a woman walked in with a man trailing behind. They were talking, but I could not hear them.

Just then, a door opened from my left, I assumed from the bedroom, and the very same woman walked in with a flourish, an older, gray-haired gentleman hot on her heels. I stopped in my tracks. I looked back at the movie, and it was mere seconds ahead of the scene acting out before me. Fascinating.

She was saying, "I certainly didn't, Mr. Dubbs. I have no idea what you are talking about." She moved over to a shiny, silver settee, lifted her lime-colored chiffon skirt from around her ankles, and sat down with an undainty plop. Her vibrant red hair slid down her bare shoulders and lay against her breast.

"You know, exactly, what I am talking about, Truline. You have got to stop with this charade!" He lifted his bowler hat from his head and tossed it on the table before the settee. "You are going to ruin your career. What kind of actress would you be if you chose to take that part?" He tapped the leg of the settee with the cane in his right hand. "Remember who your agent is, my dear. I am. And I will not allow you to go behind me and accept parts on your own. You have no idea what you are doing. I will not allow it!"

The woman, Truline, pulled a diamond earring from one ear and then the other. She tossed them on the table beside the hat. "I don't know what you are talking about, Mr. Dubbs. I have no intention of accepting any part without your knowledge. I do not know where you are getting your information from. But it simply is not true." She reached behind her neck, unclasped the matching diamond necklace, and pulled it from her throat. She tossed it absently toward the table. She missed, and it hit the floor.

Mr. Dubbs moved toward the settee and sat down beside her. He reached over and patted her knee. I moved closer to the exit but was appalled for her that he would touch her like that. Even though her dress was between her skin and his hand, it was a grotesque gesture, and I could not bear to witness it. I wanted to rush forward and do something—the cad.

"Excuse me, Sir," I said instead. "Please remove your hand from her knee." There, I said it.

Although I knew, without a doubt, that these two were ghosts, acting out some prior engagement, they both turned and looked at me. It gave me a bit of a start.

"Who are you?" Mr. Dubbs asked me directly. He stood up and stepped between me and Ms. Truline, blocking her view.

She leaned to peer around him.

"Yes, who are you?" She asked.

"Why, I am the owner of this hotel," I answered truthfully.

"You are not, Sir," Mr. Dubbs responded. "I know the owner of this hotel, but he is not you!"

I raised my chin and said, "I am the owner. I just purchased the hotel yesterday. I will not see you taking advantage of this young woman in my establishment."

Mr. Dubbs burst out laughing. "Your establishment? Sir, this hotel is owned by one Randolph Whitney. He had it built himself, just over eight years ago, in 1925." He poked his cane out in my direction. "And where did you come from? You just appeared right here in front of us. Why, I didn't even hear the door open." He took one step in my direction. "What do you mean, take advantage of her? Who do you think I am?" He questioned. "I have every right to take advantage, as you say. She owes everything to me. I am her agent."

He fired so many questions at me that I wasn't sure which to answer first. But it was "Her agent!" I exploded back at him. "You think that gives you the right to touch her with that familiarity?"

Mr. Dubbs turned and looked at Truline over his shoulder. "Do you know this man?" He barked at her.

She slid off of the settee and stepped around him to face me. "I do not know him, Mr. Dubbs. But I should like to." She smiled at me, and her eyes sparkled. A grin crept slowly onto her face.

It was the most beautiful smile, and her green eyes, which I did not fail to notice matched her dress, lit up the room. It dawned on me that she was Trueline Atherton, one of the greatest actresses of the 1930s. I remembered reading she was the most famous human being to perish in the Poland Hill Hotel just days before the fire broke out. Then, what I had read when researching this grand hotel as a child dawned on me. Truline and her lover were shot and killed in her room by her agent, Mr. Dubbs.

"Get back to your script, young lady." Mr. Dubbs spoke to her as he glared at me and tossed his cane onto the settee. He grabbed her arm to guide her back toward the bedroom. "You start filming next week." He returned to their prior conversation. "You have no time to consider other parts right now, anyway. Get this one in the can, and then we might discuss this other role. A lot of good it will do you, though. That is a role for a strumpet. Not a woman as glamorous and as beautiful as you."

He leaned toward her to kiss her cheek while he reached for the doorknob, but she pulled her arm from his grasp.

"I may owe you for finding me parts, but that does not mean you can order me around, Mr. Dubbs."

73

Her words angered him as she turned her cheek away from his searching lips.

"I've had about enough of you," He spat back at her, then turned back to me and pointed at the door. "And you, you must leave here at once, Sir."

A commotion on the wall reflecting the movie caught my attention. A young man had burst into the room from the hallway door. And just on cue, the door from the hallway burst open. The identical young man ran in and tripped over my satchel but caught himself from falling. He ran past where I stood and grabbed Mr. Dubbs by the collar. Mr. Dubbs released Truline and swung a fist at the man.

"Eddie," Truline screamed. She slid to the floor, her hand raised to cover her scream. "Eddie, stop!"

"And I've had about enough of you!" Eddie whispered into Mr. Dubbs's ear.

The newspaper had reported that Miss Truline Atherton had perished beside her lover, Mr. Edward Bowers. So this was Eddie. This was it. This was the moment Mr. Dubbs had murdered them. Hollywood had mourned her for months—a long time, actually, for Tinseltown standards.

I held my breath. Was I really about to witness what had happened that dreadful day? How had a ghost tripped over my satchel? I wanted

74

to help Eddie drag Mr. Dubbs out into the hallway but he had him soundly and capably in hand. He pulled Mr. Dubbs toward the door by the arm and collar past me. Being torn between wanting to catch a prior clue on the ever-running film or seeing the chaos in live-action, I turned and watched with amazement. Mr. Dubbs pulled a Colt Model 1903 hammerless pocket pistol from his coat pocket and blasted Eddie Bowers through the right temple. Crimson blood splattered the top half of the suite door. I felt some hit my cheek as I ducked and watched it run in rivulets down the near wall. The acrid odor of gunpowder assaulted my nose as Truline screamed. Eddie's body slowly slid to the carpet.

I rose, then stood motionless and in shock. I did nothing to stop it but watched as Mr. Dubbs whirled around and expertly shot Miss Truline Atherton, actress extraordinaire, in the face. Pieces of her skull flew out in all directions as her brain exploded out the back of her head and splashed scarlet chunks of tissue over the silver settee.

The metallic odor of blood made my stomach clinch a split second before I passed out and hit the floor.

Chapter Six

I came to find myself lying on the carpet in the sitting room of Guest suite 108. For a moment, I couldn't recollect how I had gotten here. Then, the memory returned. I sat up and looked around. The room was pristine. No blood or garish brain lingered anywhere. No film projector sat on the dresser, and my satchel was where I had dropped it. I raised to my feet and brushed off the back of my slacks. Miss Truline, Mr. Bowers, and Mr. Dubbs were nonexistent.

"Well, bugger me," I whispered to the empty room.

With my satchel now in hand, I walked to the suite door, which was white and shiny clean, opened it, and stepped out into the hallway. I wouldn't be staying in suite 108. I walked past the entrance to the spire to room 110. I twisted the knob, and this suite door opened without a key as well. What good fortune.

Suite 110 had a similar sitting room. It housed an identical silver settee. I sat down upon it to wait, the satchel at my feet, just in case something unexpected happened. Nothing did. After about fifteen minutes, I picked up my bag, walked over to the bedroom door, opened it, and went through.

I stepped back into the 1930's. Again. This room had also been decorated as yesteryear. The double bed, a majestic piece of furniture, had a high-backed headboard of pure cherry wood and a lower footboard to match. A curtain hung in the arched doorway of the clothes closet, separating it from the bedroom. I dropped my bag on the bed and hurried past to look out the window. There was my car, below and to the east of the window. I still stood in the current year.

"Whew! That gave me a start." I said aloud.

After taking a brief bath and donning clean blue jeans and a tee shirt, I crawled onto the bed and slept.

I awakened as the sun was crawling toward the west. Shadows lingered where there had been none when I lay down. I swung my feet over the side of the bed and sat up. I felt refreshed for the first time since returning to the United States two days ago. Had it only been two days? Right as rain. I dug through my satchel and pulled out a pair of trainers. My mobile phone said that it was 6:00 p.m.

After making a quick pit stop to the loo, I made my way from the suite back to the dining hall. All the tables still sat at the ready to serve the room filled with folks. The aroma of meatloaf drifted from the kitchen.

"Good evening, Molly." I watched her jump a little as if startled that anyone was in the kitchen.

"Oh, good evening, Mr. Prescott, Sir," she looked up from her pot and smiled at me. "I take it you found a good spot to rest?" She turned to face me. "I don't know why I didn't say so before, Sir, but there is a main suite on the fifth floor. I have it all ready for you. I don't know why it slipped my mind."

"Oh, I suppose that makes some sense, doesn't it, that there would be an actual room for the owner," I replied as I walked over to see what she was cooking. My stomach growled, and I realized I'd had nothing to eat since the pastry and coffee at breakfast this morning. "Oh, that does smell wonderful, Molly. What are you preparing?"

"I made you my secret meatloaf, Sir. It's in the oven, and I have these lovely glazed carrots and mashed potatoes to go with it."

"Thank you, Molly. I am ravenous."

"Of course you are, Sir. Have a seat in the dining hall, and I will get it to you shortly."

"May I assist you," I asked.

"Nonsense, Sir." She answered, wiping her hands on her pretty embroidered white apron covering her ankle-length blue cotton frock. She no longer wore the 1970's little pink uniform.

"If you insist that you have it in hand." I entered the dining hall and picked the table nearest the kitchen door.

Before long, the kitchen door opened, and I turned to watch Molly bring in the tray. But it wasn't Molly. A young woman, whom I assumed was approximately nineteen years of age, entered. The tray she held aloft appeared to be twice the circumference of herself. But she expertly maneuvered it to the side butler shelf with ease. Long blond hair, braided in a single plait to her waist, swung back and forth as she moved each plate from the tray to my table. She spoke not a word as she worked and glanced in my direction once. She had the perfect posture of British service. After placing the last plate at my left, an extraordinary bounty of assorted hard bread, she curtsied and turned to return to the kitchen.

"Hold up, please," I said, scooting my chair back and rising from the table. "Please introduce yourself," I pleaded. "My name is Alistar Prescott." I bowed at the waist toward her.

She halted at once and turned back to face me. "Oh, I know who you are, Mr. Prescott. We all do." She giggled as a young woman might and continued. "I am Elsbeth, Sir. I help Molly in the kitchen, among other things." Her cheeks were slightly flushed as she said this. "I hope your dinner is to your liking." Then she turned and moved like a gazelle back into the kitchen.

"Indeed," I picked up my napkin from the table and moved it onto my lap as I sat down.

The table was laden with more food than I could consume in a week. Six slices of meatloaf lay on one plate, accompanied by the plate of assorted bread and four additional bowls: mashed potatoes, glazed carrots, peas, candied pears, and a plate of apple pie. I had been ravenous from the moment I entered the dining hall, so it didn't take long for me to plunge through this feast.

Elsbeth had slipped in only twice to fill my glass with a beautiful red Claret. Who would have believed Claret would go so handsomely with meatloaf?

After finishing, I wiped my mouth with the napkin and placed it on the table. I rose and walked into the kitchen. No one was there.

"Molly, Elsbeth," I called out. "Thank you for the fine dinner you prepared for me." I walked through the empty kitchen, past the stove, past the sinks to look into the larder. "Hello. Anyone here?" Nope. No one was here. Where did they both skip off so quickly? I walked back to the kitchen central and realized it was immaculate. It sparkled. There was no evidence of food being prepared here recently, and no lingering scent remained. That piqued my curiosity, and I hurried back to the dining room. The table I had just vacated was bare. Well, not bare. The silverware and glassware table settings remained the same. It was as it had been before I ever entered the room.

I realized suddenly that Molly and Elsbeth had never physically been here. Had they? What jolly good fun was this? I pulled my mobile phone from my right front blue jeans pocket and hit the icon for the phone. I must tell Tom and Frankie at once. Why haven't I heard from them yet? Wasn't Tom going to call me today? What time is it now? The phone said it was 7:00 p.m. I pulled up my contact and touched Tom's face. It rang instantly. Darn, voicemail again.

Kathryn Cain

I wandered into the lobby with the phone in my hand and tried Frank next. Is no one eager to have me back in town? I couldn't believe it. Were they not as excited as I was that I had made this purchase? Had we not talked about it for years on end? I was beginning to get a little perturbed with my friends.

It dawned on me that my list of events to tell Tom and Frank was growing. Would I remember everything when I finally did reach them? I opened the Notepad app on my phone and started a new list. I titled it Notes for Tommy and Frankie. I stood looking at the blank page and wondered where to start. I would start at the beginning, of course. I turned on the microphone and began to dictate. "Upon first arriving," I paused. What happened upon first arriving? Did I see the specter in the spire, or had I awoken with that mother and her infant? I couldn't remember. Why couldn't I remember? Was that only yesterday? I would have to reflect on that later. I closed the app and put the phone in my pocket.

There was a distant growling of my stomach, which I ignored. Was there something I ate that was beginning to make me queasy?

I looked around the lit-up lobby. What to do now? I had been eager to return to the hallway off the kitchen. You know, that one which led in a downward footpath toward the back of the hotel, down into the earth to end up in that work room. The workroom with the swollen, stuck door. The one with the Irish lad. The leprechaun clown fellow.

81

Nope. I was not going there tonight. I will go there in the bright light of the morning. Windows or not, just the knowledge of sunlight outside would be a comfort. A shiver started in my toes and raced up my spine. Yes. I would leave that door for a different day.

What was that? Did I hear music? I spun on my heel and looked up at the four floors above me. The golden brass banisters sparkled above my head. But yes, there was music. I could hear it. Did Molly perhaps prepare the main bedroom suite for me this evening? She told me she had prepared it earlier, but did she turn on a radio to welcome me to the room?

I hurried to the north staircase and raced up the plush burgundy-colored carpeted steps. I raced down the hallway to the floor's northwest corner and located the stairwell leading up to the following three floors. When I stopped at the top, on the fifth floor, my lungs felt as if they were on fire. My heart beat soundly within my chest. I stumbled from the stairwell, grasped the nearest brass guardrail before me, and bent over at the waist as my chest heaved in deep breaths. The dizziness began to wane, and the shaking in my knees started to subside. My hands had become damp, and I wiped them absently on my tee shirt. It crossed my mind that I had just recently thought I needed to get into better shape. I still did. I righted myself and chuckled at my out-of-shape body. When had I become so out of shape? I had just jogged three miles the day before taking the plane from London. It had only been two days without exercise. I placed my hand over my now slow heart and retuned my ears to listen, again, for the sound of music.

There it was, so faint, floating on the air like a breeze. It instantly calmed me, like a chantress stills my soul. I followed that sound from the corner where I stood by the stairwell toward the opposite corner. But there was no corner. The hallway abruptly stopped when it reached the south wall. The entire fifth floor was just this one north-south hallway at the west end of the hotel. I had not noticed from below that the fifth-floor hallway balustrade did not skirt the entire building like the other floors. I turned around and walked back to the center of the hall. I found myself in front of a double-door suite. Suite number 515. How had I passed this room without seeing it? I spun around and looked out across the open space above the lobby to the opposite side of the building. This suite was the only room in this hallway and was the entire fifth floor. The lilting sound behind these doors was mesmerizing, and I felt like it had lulled me to come here. Was I really that predictable? I had not come of my own accord. I realized I had made the exact opposite decision to stay in room 110, where I had napped and where my satchel still resided.

The suite doors were light blue rather than the white of the previous floors. Each door had a doorknocker, and each contained a peephole. Had I noticed knockers and peepholes in the lower doors? I couldn't remember offhand.

Now, I have always prided myself on the almost perfect recall capabilities of my memory. It has always been my most prized characteristic. I can recall conversations from years ago nearly verbatim. Between my practically total recall and the ability of my natural perspicacious nature, which was also a trait that made me excel, I became a well-spoken-after Barrister in England. People came from all over the country to seek out my services. I remembered law cases as clear as every story I had ever heard about this house on Poland Hill. Why could I not remember what happened first, only yesterday?

The light blue double doors opened beneath the soft touch of my hands and swung inward smoothly on well-oiled hinges. The wafting, fragrant scent of fresh-cut flowers instantly caused me to sneeze. The overhead light was on, and the room was warm and welcoming. It beckoned me closer with the sounds of fire licking, popping, and crackling logs inside a welcoming colossal stone fireplace. I entered at once and walked directly to the firebox. It appeared to be etched directly into the wall. The same white marble as the lobby floor and support columns below made up the mantle and hearth, and I ran my hand over the mantles' delightfully smooth finish.

Kathryn Cain

Upon the mantle sat a beautiful radio direct from The Golden Age of Radio, the 1930's. From this radio emanated the sound of the music I heard. However, the lilting sound I recognized as music from the 1933 film Footlight Parade flowed through the room sharply and clearly. I had recognized the tune from the hallway. My Nan listened to it constantly, and after having watched it with her several times, I remember it starred James Cagney and Joan Blondell, Ruby Keeler, and Dick Powell. I guess my memory is still intact despite my inability to focus on the events of yesterday.

The chimney rose half in front and half inside the wall. I reached out and touched the stones as I looked up to view its' height. This fifth-floor room had a much higher ceiling than the lower-floor guest rooms. Upon its ecru-colored stones hung a beautiful oil painting. It was a painting of the old hotel where I now found myself. The view looked at the manor from the south lawn. I recognized the window from the pub on the first-floor level. It was the window where I witnessed, just this morning, the patrons watching the horse race on a track that was no longer in existence. To the left of the window, the tower shaft rose, leading to the spire. And to the left of the tower, almost as if someone had added it to the original painting at a much later date, was a glass room hovering several floors above the ground. What on earth was that?

I looked over my shoulder to the left. The adjoining bedroom door stood wide open. I took another glance at the mysterious painting and hurried into the bedroom. The room did not contain the standard 1930s double bed but a king-size bed on a black wrought iron frame, complete with black iron head and footboards. I determined the old guy, Wilbur Hamilton, had at least updated and redecorated this room for himself. The south wall of the bedroom was complete with twin glass French doors, which led to an outside sitting room. I couldn't wait to see the view and hurried out. The sitting room hung five stories above the south lawn. And, as the painting attested, the rooms' walls were made entirely of glass. A curved window carved through the southern wall was a brilliant monument of glass and stone. A window seat was ensconced within. The top half of the window was louvered out, and a cool breeze blew in. In front of the window seat, a leather recliner sat facing the window. The only other furniture in this small room was a small table resting on the right side of the armchair. I could picture Mr. Hamilton seated here, a book nestled in his lap with a glass of bourbon near at hand sitting on the table. Now, this was the room I needed to make my own. Molly had been right. I was glad she had made it ready for me.

I glanced around the little glass enclosure to ensure there were electrical plugs I could make use of for my computer and mobile phone and was delighted to see Mr. Hamilton had ensured there were. I laughed a surprisingly giddy giggle. My mind discovered it to be a bit manic, but I didn't give it any more thought, so I turned back through the bedroom to the sitting room. I don't know how long I stood in front of that warm fire, staring at the painting that hung there. But when I realized I was heating up pretty good the sun had begun to set.

Chapter Seven

It didn't take me long to grab my belongings and move into the room on the fifth floor. I stayed in there the rest of the evening listening to the radio, which only seemed to be playing music from the 1930s. I pondered long and hard about how that could happen. Of course, the only thing that I could come up with was that the radio itself was haunted. I left it on, closed the glass doors to the fireplace, and climbed under the covers of the king-size bed. It was warm and cozy, and it didn't take me long to drift off to sleep.

Voices outside my suite door awakened me after only a brief time. They were loud enough to hear over the fifth rendition of Stormy Weather (Keeps Rainin' All The Time) by Ethel Waters. I threw back the covers, flung my legs over the side of the bed, stood, and grabbed my robe from the foot of the bed. I shrugged into it and tripped over the hanging bedspread on my way to the door. I couldn't imagine what was going on. I flung open the suite's double doors.

"What is the meaning of all this noise," I asked as I stepped out into the hallway. "It's so early," I complained out loud.

The hallway was empty, but the sound was outrageously loud. I stepped up to the brass railing and looked down at the lobby. I instinctively jumped back a foot, then leaned forward to peer down again, hoping not to be seen. There was bedlam on the lobby floor.

There must have been thirty or forty apparitions, some solid, some mere whiffs resembling smoke or mist wafting across the floor. I jumped further back when one such wraith flew up directly in front of me. Its black maw opened hideously, and I was sure my head would be swallowed in one horrific bite, yet it only howled in my face. I hit my head on the wall behind me, my mouth open in a silent scream. The presence turned abruptly and soared to my right, only to swoop straight back at me before plunging back down to the lobby.

I tiptoed back to the guardrail and peered down. The chaos had not subsided. Ghosts in all forms filled the open space before me. It was not without note the more solid ones donned an array of clothing styles that spanned many centuries. There, a woman who would have been at home on the seat of a covered wagon and beside her, a young woman who wore only a string bikini. How was this possible when the Poland Hill fire had been in 1934? It didn't make any sense.

Yet, I was exhilarated. I started to turn toward the stairs to join them in the lobby when I realized one thing. They had all turned their faces, well, those who had faces, up to stare directly at me.

"What the...?"

I then realized the din included actual words, and I strained to listen. What were they saying? They all talked or howled over each other, and it was hard to decipher. Suddenly, it came to me. They were all talking to me.

"Welcome home."

"So good to see you again."

"What took you so long?"

"Where have you been?"

The questions kept flying at me. What were they saying? Good to see me again. When had they seen me before?

"You have to leave."

"Yes, this is our house."

"No, he has to stay."

"He can't leave. Who will make sure we have a place to live if he leaves?"

They turned to look at each other, and I couldn't believe it. The ghosts began to argue.

"Wait one moment," I said, wagging my finger at them. "I will come right down."

I ran to the stairs, my robe sailing out behind me, and took the steps two at a time. By the time I got down to the lobby level, I was out of breath, and my legs wobbled. I stopped at the bottom of the staircase to catch my breath. The spirits swarmed around me, and the unexpected silence was deafening.

All I could do was stare at them for a moment as they stood or wafted in front of me.

"Well, now. That's better." I said. "What's this all about?" I was talking to ghosts. Suppose Frankie and Tommy could see me now. I had hoped to find a few spirits on this estate, but indeed not this many.

One male, who had once been a live and handsome man, stepped up to me. Flesh bubbled red and raw upon his face. He turned and looked at the others. "There's naught can be done now. He can't help us any more than the last chap. That Wilbur Hamilton." He turned and looked back at me. "You can't help us. No one can."

"I'm not sure what you are asking. How do you need help? What do you need me to do?" I genuinely wanted to help. Was that what I had wanted all along? There was movement to my left, and the specter from last night, the woman who held her dead infant, walked over to me and raised the child toward me.

"Oh, I'm sorry," I sighed, and a tear welled up in my eye as I watched one slide down her face. "I wish I could do something." I looked over the crowd before me. "I can't."

She clutched her child close, turned, and walked away.

Another woman, her hair singed short and wearing clothes that appeared to be smoking, said, "I told you he couldn't do anything."

"Give him a chance," an old man in a wheelchair piped.

"He wouldn't know how," the smoking lady said.

"Yes, give him a chance," a towheaded boy of about seventeen agreed.

"Tell me what you want me to do," I pleaded. "Tell me how." I tried to sort out all the voices as they all started to talk at once. I was astounded that many believed there was something that I could do for them. "What is it?" I asked again."

But as I watched, one by one, they all began to fade. "Wait," I beseeched them, "tell me what you want me to do."

And just like that, they were gone. What a conundrum. I stared at that empty lobby for a long time. Wishing for them to return. They didn't.

"Blimey, that's just jolly good, isn't it?" I scratched the top of my head.

I glanced around the room, trying to determine what I would now do. Sleeping was definitely out of the question at this point. All of these ghosts seemed to be nice, ordinary people, certainly not like that malevolent, evil, nasty leprechaun of a clown down in the gardening tool room. I remember how he bobbed up and down in front of me, and a shiver ran up my spine. I realized that I was frigid. I looked down and saw I was standing on the marble floor in my bare feet. I had not put on my slippers.

I turned and looked four flights above me at my suite. I wondered if the fireplace still had a spark. I didn't think I could cut the mustard to retake those stairs. My feet would have to bear the chill.

I headed toward the kitchen, hoping Molly or Elsbeth might have left a kettle on the stove. Maybe one of them could give me some insight into the events of the night. The kitchen was dark and empty. I turned the lights on. No kettle lingered here, so I grabbed one from the butler's pantry, along with a can of tea, filled it with water, and lit the stove. I found a cup and sat down at the kitchen table to wait. It didn't take long for the water to boil. My thoughts were held captive by the appearance of the crowd tonight, and I could not rid them from my mind. There was a clock on the counter, and I was surprised to see that it was 5:00 in the morning. Didn't ghosts show up at midnight in most stories? I guess mine are late sleepers. I had a chuckle on that one. I was a mixed-up mess. I was laughing and totally distraught at the same instant. I drank my tea, but it did not soothe me. I can not express to you how useless I felt at that moment. The most useless I had ever been in my entire life to date.

Upon realizing that I had not searched the north side of the lobby, I left my tea cup and saucer sitting on the table and went directly there. And, lo and behold, behind the sweeping north staircase was another room. Its doors stood open wide, and above them hung a wooden sign with the word "Library" inscribed upon it. My lucky day, night, morning.

I was thrilled to find the floor covered in the same lush, warm burgundy carpeting as the stairs. My toes welcomed the change. The walls were all lined with built-in mahogany bookshelves, etched in gold laurel with vintage Baroque brass scrolled décor ornamentation. The shelves reached the ceiling on all sides. Each wall contained a ladder that ran on a rail below the uppermost shelf. It was glorious, to be sure. Being the intellect I believe I am, books are one of the most important aspects of my life. I found myself in heaven. The scent of dried leather-bound books filled the space with warmth and familiarity. Six leather armchairs took center stage in the room and surrounded a knee-high circular table. The room contained two large windows surrounded by bookshelves that, in daylight, looked out over the north garden. Each had two leather high-backed armchairs facing them with a small table nestled between them. Scattered about were five small desks with hard-backed chairs. Ones as you might use in a university classroom. The ambiance was one of style and comfort. The very best library a fine hotel might offer to its patrons. I settled into a circular pattern, studying the titles of books and names of authors as I passed. It was impossible to see them all. There were leather-bound tomes, hardcover volumes, and paper-backs. There were old ones from the 1920s and newer ones from the late 1960s. So many fine publications.

My circuit moved me closer to one of the university-style desks, and I noticed it held a stack of hardbacked volumes. A tall stack. There must have been fifteen or so. I glanced at the titles almost as an afterthought. Then I swept some from the top of the stack onto the desk and looked further down the pile. My eyes grew wide. What was this? They were all about ghosts. Every single one of them. *Living with Spirits, The Unseen Friend, A Resolute Soul,* and *The Presence Within,* to name a few. Who had stacked these here? Of course, it had to be Wilbur Hamilton. He had seen them, too. They had wanted him to help them years before me until the authorities dragged him from this place, a screaming, blathering, broken man. I pulled the chair away from the desk a bit too abruptly, lifted my robe, and sat in a newly found frenzy. He had been on to something. What was it?

I shuffled the volumes around to some order and yanked open the desk drawer to look for a writing utensil and paper. I stopped at once. There, on top of a stack of clean notepads, lay a spiral notebook. Written on the cover with a bold hand, "WFH." Wilbur Ferdinand Hamilton. He had been researching information about my new friends in residence. I opened the notebook to the first written page. The writing was sure and firm, if not a bit pretentious, but as I flipped through pages and pages of writing, the hand became messy. Giant letters swept across the final pages in haste and what must have been fear. His words made no sense in the end. Poor dear old chap.

I turned back to the first page and began to read. He started with some of the same questions as I had. Why was the house haunted by so many? Of course, there had been the fire in 1934, but there were spirits here from far before and far after that horrid fateful day, as proven by the young woman in the bikini and the women with the bonnets, the one who looked like she belonged in a covered wagon and the mother with the dead infant. Why were they drawn to this place? We were in the middle of South Carolina, for Heaven's sake. Why would spirits from all ages mingle here? It didn't take long for me to get to a page where Mr. Hamilton mentioned the apparition in the cellar. His letters screamed off the page as I read them. His experience had been identical to mine. The word CLOWN leaped at me. I had worked very hard to escape the memory from yesterday evening. But there it was. Thank you for that reminder, Mr. Hamilton. I sat back and put the notebook back in the drawer where it belonged. I would come to read more later.

I had not noticed the sun had begun its rise to light the room. My stomach growled, and I rose to go and look for a snack when a sound interrupted me. I looked over to the left window, expecting to see a bird that might have accidentally struck it, but there was none. To my surprise, a man rose from an armchair upon which he had been hidden from my view.

"Oh, dear God!" My hand flew to my mouth, should I perhaps express more. "How long have you been there?" How could I not have passed him in my prior circuitry of the room?

"Good day, Alister," he responded.

"You know me," I said.

"But of course," he answered. He was about six foot three inches tall, bald as a ball in a game of billiards, and looked uncannily familiar to me. "You were in my sixth-grade history class before you left so quickly to return to England that summer. I enjoyed you immensely and was looking forward to having you in seventh-grade history."

"My sixth-grade class?" I stepped around the desk and moved closer to him. The sunlight was getting brighter by the window where he stood. "Oh, blimey!" I said. "You're Mr. Abernathy. You're Mr. Abernathy, aren't you?" What good fortune. I had enjoyed Mr. Abernathy. He was one of the most brilliant teachers and was solely behind my love of learning. I would have recognized him immediately had he sported more hair.

"Yes, yes," he continued, "I am Mr. Abernathy. And look at you! Look at what you have become. Why, one of the best attorneys around, I hear."

"Thank you, Mr. Abernathy." I was extremely pleased to see him. "How nice of you to say. Although, I have retired now."

"Retired? Why, you are what, maybe forty-two perhaps?"

"Yes, forty-two exactly," I answered. "I was very fortunate to put enough away." Then I thought, "But you knew my parents, didn't you?"

"Yes, yes. Nice people."

"Well, they died ten years ago. They left me quite a bit of money since they had also inherited a great deal from Granddad." I felt like a bloody fool. Shame swelled that I had not earned that money. "And what about you, Mr. Abernathy? What are you doing here?" Then it dawned on me he was dead. Mr. Abernathy was a ghost. But my question still stood. What was he doing here, in this house?

He stepped around the armchair and walked toward me with his hand out. "Ned. It's just Ned. Mr. Abernathy was that old school teacher." He laughed. "I don't have to go by Mr. Abernathy anymore."

I shook his hand. And I did shake his hand. It was firm, the skin soft but solid. I did not flinch when cold seeped into my hand. "How do you come to find yourself here?" I asked again.

"I don't exactly know the answer to that question, Alister," he rubbed his chin as he looked at the floor. "I have been trying to figure that out myself. I went to bed one night about six years ago and woke up here. Of course, I immediately knew where I was even though I had never stepped foot in this place before. Just like you, I was raised in town and knew all the stories. All those rumors." He laughed out loud, remembering those stories. "Although I hadn't believed them like you did back in the day. But, here I am, and now I do." He chuckled again. "Funny thing, isn't it?"

My stomach growled again. Loud enough for both of us to hear.

"Come on, I'll walk with you to the kitchen, get you something to eat. It's pretty early, but I'm sure Molly will be around."

"You know Molly?" I asked incredulously. Then I laughed along with him. He didn't need to answer. Of course, he knew Molly.

Chapter Eight

We sat at the kitchen table while Molly refilled my coffee cup. My fresh pastry quickly became just a memory. I wished I had eaten one more. The hole in my stomach was yet unfilled.

"It was that nefarious creature in the cellar," Ned continued. "That's what broke him, I think. I hear he was a nice old man. From the old stories, yes, but also from the others. I didn't know him myself, but that's what they all say. The ones who were here before him."

"I can understand how that could happen. I'm pretty freaked out about the bloke as well." I gave an involuntary shudder thinking about it. "I do want to know where that door leads, but not bad enough to chance running into him again. I had a lot of trouble sleeping Friday night. I haven't had nightmares like that since childhood." I slugged down the final half of my coffee, and I jumped as Molly appeared on my left to refill my cup.

"That's where they found Mr. Hamilton, you know. Down in that cellar in front of that door. Blithering like an idiot. Going on and on about that damn clown." Molly's appearance had not affected him in the least, and Ned shook his head and said, "I don't understand it. How can folks be so scared of a clown? Why, when I was a kid, my parents took me three times to The Ringling Brothers Barnum and

Bailey Circus when they came to Charleston. They called it the Greatest Show on Earth. There were clowns galore. I wasn't afraid of them then, and I'm not afraid of them now." He watched me take another sip of my coffee. "I sure do miss a good cup of joe in the mornings." He licked his lips and continued, "That guy down there, he's been here the longest of any of us. Word is he was alone for a lot of years. Rumor has it he was an actual clown when he was alive."

"You're telling me even ghosts have rumors?" I chuckled uneasily.

"You wouldn't believe the number of clatterfarts. Now, do you want to hear this or not?" Ned Abernathy was never one to mince words. "Our ghost-clown worked for The Hagenbeck-Wallace Circus. They went all over the country puttin' on their shows, until one day, June 22, 1918, to be exact, they were in a terrible crash. All loaded up on a train, they were. When some engineer, running a train full of troops, fell asleep and ran his train right into the back of the circus train. Eighty-six people were killed, and one hundred and twenty-seven injured. It went down as one of the worst train wrecks in U.S. history. Happened near Hammond, Indiana. Now, that's over eight hundred miles away. Not sure how he got here back in 1918. That was before they even broke ground on this place. So your guess is as good as mine. But he's been here ever since. But then I don't even know how I got here myself, and I lived right here in town." He leaned forward and whispered, "And, yes, we ghosts have rumors. It's heard that his name is Patrick Monaghan. Guess that's why he reminds us of a leprechaun. Good ole' Irish boy he was. Hear talk he was the star of the show, Pat the Clown. Wonder how he got so angry."

I had a thought but was winging it, "Was the amusement park here then?" I leaned forward over my cup to peer into Ned's face, looking for anything.

Ned looked me straight in the eye and winked, "You know, you are right about that. The amusement park was here then. It opened in the summer of 1915. Ten years prior to this mansion. The swimming pool and health spas opened the summer after the park. Interesting thought, Alister." He grinned.

"Why would he come here to the amusement park? And if he died in 1918 and was the first of your kind here, how are there ghosts here from prior time periods? That doesn't make any sense." I couldn't begin to understand where this was leading.

"I don't know why he came here. But I do know this. Those folks came after him, and that old door, the one down in the cellar, leads down the ridge of the hill and comes out beside the hot springs, right beside that amusement park."

"Well, I'll be." I sat back in my chair. "He's blocking the way to the park. Why is he doing that?"

"I have no idea, but he has kept all of us from going through. Not just old Wilbur Hamilton." Ned looked at my coffee cup and licked his lips again but shook his head. "I have no idea, but I think we should find out." He scooted his chair back, stood up, and clapped his hands with excitement. "I love a good adventure!"

I didn't know I would feel such relief to hear Ned say that. Even if he was dead, I was no longer alone.

After arranging to meet at the back of the kitchen in fifteen minutes, I ran up to my room to get dressed. I wished old Mr. Hamilton had put in a lift, but I flew up the steps eager and excited.

I dressed in my usual retirement clothes, consisting of blue jeans and a tee shirt. This one was short-sleeved and navy blue. I slid into my trainers and grabbed my phone from the charger on the bedside table. I was surprised to see that it was 8:00 in the morning. I had somehow wiled away four hours since rising. It was Sunday. I had only been here two nights. It felt like it had been a week.

I flew down the carpeted stairs two at a time, yet something coaxed me to stop on the third floor. I hesitated on the step above the floor, wrestling between my plan to meet Ned in the kitchen as agreed and the desire to investigate what was calling to me. I found myself standing in front of suite 315 before I knew I had made my decision. 315. Two floors below my room.

Laughter, accompanied by the sounds of glasses clinking, escaped into the hall. The stench of cigarette smoke tingled my nose. I had no thought of knocking. The doorknob turned quietly, and I opened the door just wide enough to peek in.

The sitting room was large enough to accommodate a burning fireplace, two high-backed leather armchairs placed before it, and one immense, extremely long, white linen-covered table. Three two-foot tall candelabras, each with five two-foot black candles, lit the table. Ten men and women clothed in their 1920s finery were seated around it. They sat stick rod straight and proper, four to a side; a woman and man, assumed to be the hosts, at the ends. The men all dressed alike, tucked into black long-tailed tuxedos with white shirts and white bow ties. The women, adorned in sparkled jewels and sequined silks of pinks and burgundies, grays, blues, and silvers, held a glimmer of individuality. Two female servers were in attendance.

I noticed a magazine on a small table beside the door and to my right. Opened on the center page, it was instantly familiar. The very scene taking place before me was the object of the two-page spread. The celebrants' movements were mimicked instantly in the photograph. I was astounded by the likeness.

Looking back to the room, I was startled to witness twelve faces turn to stare at me simultaneously. Bird carnival masks adorned each face. It was a flock of gold and gilt, silver and sparkles, hawk, crow, and owl beaks, peacock feathers, and plumage that stared at me with curiosity. It was a stunning array, and I had intruded into their private celebration. However, I opened the door a bit wider to get a fuller view of the beauty before me.

The female servers, dressed in black uniform dresses, stood at each table end. The server on my left, her white apron stained with blood, stood patiently, a large silver serving tray in her outstretched right hand arrested while serving the woman, who was draped entirely in strings of pearls, seated at the end of the banquet table. Revulsion stabbed me when I saw the offerings held aloft upon the tray. Steaming lumps of bloody red body organs sat ready to be selected. The pearled woman's fork, held aloft, prepared to stab what appeared to be a human heart. Bowls filled with bubbling and unidentifiable foods sat before each guest. Ichor seeped over the sides as they steamed in plumes of green and yellow. Plates littered the table with an assortment of finger foods that I would not dare touch with my own hand. I could not even determine the treats they bore.

The second server held a silver tray twice the size of the other. It was piled high with a dozen gift boxes decorated in colors, gold, silver, and ribbons as beautifully as the masked attendees. The boxes lifted themselves in an ever-swirling frenzy, flipping their places as they tumbled over each other in a shimmering display. It was magic. I glanced down at the magazine spread and saw that they did the same. I stood transfixed by the visions before me. I finally focused my eyes on the serving woman to the left. Her long blonde braid flowed over her left shoulder, her golden owl mask asking the perpetual question, Who? Elsbeth.

The man seated at the right end of the table rose and walked toward me, his hawk beak bobbing up and down, his white shirt blotted with blood.

Caught in a moment of nightmare-gripping fear, a sudden feeling I had overindulged, against my will, in drugs and alcohol, nausea welled up within me. My knees buckled, and I dropped to the floor. The hawk man reached the door, nodded at me, then closed it and shut me out.

I rose to my knees and threw up on the beautifully ornate hallway carpet. I pulled myself to my feet using the hallway railing and regained a steady foot. I inhaled deep lungs full of fresh hallway air. The closed doors of suite 315 did not belie what lay within. It was not lost on me that this horrid meal was taking place just after 8:00 in the morning. My time, of course. I had no idea what time or year was taking place inside that room.

Remembering I had a previous date, I limped to the staircase and, with my hand pressing upon my cramping belly, descended to the first floor.

I reached the kitchen entrance and looked around for Ned. He was nowhere to be seen. I had arrived before him. I am not sure how that happened. I was engaged, even dreadfully so, at the dinner party above and arrived later than our prearranged time. Who knew what could have kept Ned from being here before me? Did ghosts get distracted as I had done? I reached the kitchen center without running into Molly or Elsbeth. Well, I knew where Elsbeth was, though, didn't I? I knew it was still early, but hadn't Molly told me there was to be a Gala for me this evening? A party in celebration and honor of my return to town? Molly had said everyone was excited that I was back. I would have expected her to be working on food preparation of some sort. However, if they expected so many, they might have the food ordered and catered in. What was I thinking? Ghosts couldn't order in food. Could they? I had witnessed they were able to do a great many things.

I walked around to the back of the kitchen, where Ned and I agreed to meet, but it was also empty. I pulled the phone from my jeans pocket and saw it was only 8:15 a.m. My stop at room 315 had been mere moments of horror. I had a frantic moment of panic when the trauma of the room hit me again, and I rushed to chunder into a dustbin sitting beside the back door. I wiped spittle from my lips with the bottom of my tee shirt and looked up. A back door. The kitchen had a back door located beside the door to the butler pantry. Why hadn't I seen that before? It had no window in it, but it should lead out to the west side of the mansion. If that were so, then it would lead to the gravel road I saw from the tower. It led to the north crest of the hill, then down to the pools and the park. Eager to see the road and, hence, confirm the ability to enter the park without running into that devil clown again, I was all for it. I would peek out the door only for a minute for confirmation while I awaited Ned.

I stepped to the door and found it locked. Why would it be locked? I would think it a fire hazard, at the very least. Had they learned nothing since the fire of 1934? Of course, other than Wilbur Hamilton, it has stood empty since then. Ghosts don't need unlocked doors, do they? I would need to remedy that for myself. The most logical place to check for a key was the butler's pantry. I stepped through the doorway, and an inkling led me to reach up to the top left shelf behind the opened door. My hand came away with a brass key enclosed within. I hurried back to the kitchen door, and miracle upon miracle, the brass key fit into the keyhole with perfection. I wiggled it a bit, the lock caught, and the key turned. I opened the door.

It was a September morning. 8:20 a.m. I expected to open the door to sunlight. It was pitch black. I stared out the door, perplexed. Sunrise is typically around 7:00 a.m. this time of year. Even with an overcast, cloudy morning, there would be light. There was none. Not a speck. Not a sliver. Black. I slammed the door shut. What deception was this? Confusion clouded my brain. I made no sense of it. I opened the door for another quick peek and slammed it shut again. Bewilderment. Then, my brain started to work, and I ran back to the butler's pantry in search of a real torch. I found one and returned post haste to the phantom door. I turned the torch on. It didn't work. I turned it into my face and shook it. I knew the batteries must be ancient and shouldn't work. But they did, and it blinded me for an instant. Bloody fool. I turned to the door, torch at the ready, and slowly opened. I stuck the torch outside an instant before my head. I was dumbfounded. The door opened into a cave. A small, dark cave. The back wall was no more than thirty feet from the door. The sides reached only about fifteen feet on either side. Settled on the rocky floor were three rows of wooden folding chairs. The sort you might sit upon at a card table. Small, seemingly flimsy, yet solid. Set in what looked like a specific pattern, there were six chairs in the first row, with two sets of three behind them and a space of four between them. The third row held four chairs behind the space of the second row. They were assembled like this:

XXXX

XXX   XXX

XXXXXX

It was an unusual display. Sixteen chairs, sitting in the dark, in a small cave beyond a door I was sure did not exist when I had visited the butler's pantry before.

I lifted my foot to cross the threshold when a voice said, "I wouldn't do that if I were you." Startled, I stopped and looked over my shoulder. Ned stood beside me and shook his head. "Look there," he pointed down just beyond my feet.

I looked where he was pointing. A twenty-foot-wide fissure split the cavern floor between me and the first row of chairs. I shone the torch into the fissure, and no light bounced back.

"Bloody hell," I bent down on one knee and swung the torch to and fro. "How deep does it go?" I looked up at Ned. "What are these chairs for? What is this place?"

Ned knelt and joined me to look down into the massive crack. "I have no idea. I have never seen this before. A bit strange, isn't it?"

"It's for the witches." Molly stood behind us.

"The witches?" I asked.

"Yes, the witches. Kept them here, they did." She grabbed us both by the arm and pulled us away from the door. Then she walked around us and closed it.

"I don't understand," I didn't understand.

I followed as Molly led us back to the table where we had sat only an hour and a half ago. This time, she sat down with us.

"I was one of them," Molly continued. "Well, I wasn't a witch, but they thought I was." She leaned forward and put her elbows on the table, hands clasped before her, but she gave us a little wink. "I got no trial. The townsfolk thought I was a witch and cast me into that cave with four other women. Left us there. No food, no water. In the dark. Stayed there 'til we died. That was it."

Ned and I looked at each other and then back at Molly. I couldn't help but think of Elsbeth upstairs, the tray of steaming organs in her hand, and what suddenly looked like a ritual taking place. Molly tugged that thought right out of my head.

"The first one died within four days. Her name was Mary. She was the wife of the preacher. I don't know why they would turn against dear Mary. Frail little thing she was. She didn't stand a chance against them. Cried the entire time, poor dear. I think she went first because she shed all those tears. Couldn't keep the water inside of her. You think ghosts are scary. Look at the living. Horrible lot.

Sarah was the second to go. She lasted five days. Married to the Haberdasher. She was the oldest of us. Why, I think she was going on fifty years. Such a shame that. Old Mr. Whitley couldn't stop them. Pleaded with them, he did. Dropped onto his knees while they dragged her, screaming, out of his shop. Pityful display. He loved her much, I think.

Prudence and Alice died the very next day. I don't know much about them. They didn't talk much. Just sat there clinging to each other, they did. I did overhear Alice came from Massachusetts. Don't know why they brought her all the way here. Traveling was hard in those days. Not like today." She sat back and looked at us, then sighed and went on, "I lasted the longest. Sat there for three more days. Couldn't see their bodies, but I sure could detect the stench of them. I came to figure out if they really were witches and not innocent like me, they would have gotten themselves out of there. Not sat and died like that. That's what I figure."

Molly stood up and walked over to a shelf, stopped at the stovetop, then set three cups on the table and poured them full of hot coffee. I picked mine up, took a heavenly whiff, and sipped. I looked at them over the rim of my cup. They hung their heads over the steam and inhaled.

"Nothing," Ned looked at her.

"Me, too," Molly answered. "It was worth another try."

They both took to laughing so hard that Ned nearly fell off of his chair. I was glad they could look at their situation so gleefully. I don't know how I would behave if I died and was stuck here.

"I am so sorry to hear about that, Molly." I placed the cup back on the table, feeling remorse for their inability to have coffee and by Molly's story. "It must have been awful for you."

"Oh, don't you worry about that, dear. I am much happier now than I was before. Look at this place I get to live in." She waved her arm around the kitchen. "I may not get to eat the food, but I sure do enjoy preparing it. I am happy to have someone to cook for again."

Ned nodded in agreement. "It's good to have you here, Alister. I have been missing intelligent conversation." He patted the back of Molly's hand, "No offense, Molly dear."

"Oh, none taken, Ned. You have much more knowledge about things than I do. I know that."

"It's good to know that after you die, you can still have mates, uh, friends," I smiled at them. "And, thinking of friends..." I pulled my phone out of my jeans and looked at it. 9:00 a.m. already. "I have been expecting a call this morning from at least one friend. No one yet." Wait, it's Sunday. Didn't Tom say he would call me yesterday? Wonder what happened there? "So, Ned, what do you have planned for the cellar?"

"I guess I got distracted. We need to get back to the library. See what we can do about ole Pat The Clown." He stood up and carried his cup to the sink. "Molly, if you will excuse us, we have a clown who needs to be taken care of."

Molly rose and followed with her cup. "Oh, you boys, go right ahead. I have to get ready for a gala tonight, don't I."

I smiled at that. I will see Tom and Frank tonight.

Chapter Nine

Ned and I stepped into the library and immediately took our seats. He wanted to go over his plan to get rid of pesky Pat.

I quickly started firing questions at him. "I don't understand why he is blocking the door," I said. "Why would he keep you from going through? Couldn't you find any other way around?" I was thinking of that drive that went on the west side of the house. "Can you go out of the house? Why doesn't he want anyone to get to the amusement park? What will we find there?"

Ned laughed heartily. "Slow down, young man. So many questions, and I don't have an answer for any of them, except the one about leaving the house. Yes, we can leave the house. We just can't leave the hill. I don't know who made those rules. But that's the fact of it."

"So why don't we just go out the front door and take the car down the drive that leads to the park?" Seemed plausible to me.

"I don't think it is that easy, son." Ned's face hinted at indecisiveness.

"If you can go outside, why isn't it that easy?"

"Well, it just isn't. That's all."

"That's the kind of answer I used to get from my parents. I'm forty-two, Ned. Give it up."

"It's not that, Alister. I've tried it. About three years ago. I went out from the Prancing Pony and around the building, past the kitchen entrance and over to the crest of the hill. I walked across the grass. Didn't take the drive. Doesn't matter, tried the drive later. Hit a brick wall. Well, it felt like a brick wall. But there was nothing there. I couldn't see a thing there. Have you ever heard of a ghost who couldn't walk through walls? Well, that's what happened. I hit that wall hard. If I wasn't already dead, I think I would have broken my foot. Toe, at least."

"Well, that certainly is interesting."

"Yep. That's what I thought. I asked Molly to try. Same wall. Then I asked some of the guys in the Prancing Pony. A bunch of us tried." He scratched his head as if thinking. "We never figured it out. I wonder if it has anything to do with the clown. We never considered that."

"Now I have to try it." I got excited and jumped to my feet. "What if it is only you ghosts who can't go through." I ran for the library door.

Ned yelled after me, "You can try it, my friend. But I have to watch." He ran after me.

We cleared the front steps without incident. I ran swiftly and surely. Ned decided to soar down in a stunning display of finesse, missing the steps entirely. I laughed excitedly, and I felt like I was back at twelve years old. I couldn't wait to get to the crest of the hill.

Feeling snarky, I said, "Bet you can't beat me there!" I ran as fast as I could. Thank heavens I had kept up with my health and fitness. I ran at full throttle without losing my breath. I rounded the southwest corner, between the house and the large tool shed, and came to a complete stop. Ned was standing at the crest of the hill, right arm out straight, wrist flexed, his flat hand pushing against nothing. He leaned there, bald head glistening in the sunlight, an outrageously massive grin on his face.

Exploding with laughter, I took off to catch up to him. "You cheated!" I shouted to him.

"Of course, I didn't cheat. How would I cheat?" Ned knocked on the invisible wall. The rapping echoed and quivered like tapping onto an empty metal drum. "What do you think of this?"

He knocked on the wall again, and I covered my ears as I approached him. "It certainly is loud." I reached out and touched the wall. "Well, I can feel it too. Strange. It feels like a cold steel."

"What did I tell you?"

"You're right. I had to see it to believe it. No pun intended since I actually can't see it." A frown creased my brow as I ran both hands over the invisible barrier to experience the wall myself.

Then, just like Tommy did with that wrought iron fence all those years ago, I crossed the yard until I reached the copse of trees at the west ridge of the hill. I trailed my hand along the wall, no electric shock in evidence. I turned and walked back to Ned and stopped beside him. I turned to the northern ridge, hands pressed against the cool metal that I couldn't see.

"Why doesn't he want us to go down there?" It was a rhetorical question. I expected no answer. "So the only way through is through that damn clown."

"So it seems."

"I think we need to find out everything we can about this place. Before the fire and after it." That seemed a silly thing to say because I had previously thought I knew everything about this place. But, as with the tower starting on the second floor, the Prancing Pony, whose walls should have been more prominent than the south wall would allow, and the hallway leading to the cellar, I didn't know everything I believed I did. I was to learn there was a whole lot more.

I walked back to the mansion with determination. Ned walked beside me rather than doing that disappearing act he did coming outside. We headed straight to the library and to the desk with the stacks of ghost books.

"Maybe Wilbur was on to something," I pulled the drawer open and pulled out Mr. Hamilton's notes. Without sitting down and bending over the desk, we started skimming the first page. "Look here. He refers to each book and page where he found something."

"What was he looking for?" Ned asked me. "What are you thinking?"

"You should know better than I do, Ned. I'm new to this ghost business. But I was thinking there must be something in the theme park that ole' Pat doesn't want anyone to see. Didn't you say the park was here before any other ghosts started to arrive?" I looked at Ned and continued, "And didn't you say that you think Pat The Clown was the first ghost to inhabit this place? He was drawn here after the train crash. Why? He was here before anyone. Before the house on Poland Hill, this house, was ever erected? Ever dreamed about. He was drawn here before the fire! Holy cow, he was here before Trueline Atherton died. Do you think he had a hand in Mr. Dubbs shooting her and Eddie Bowers?" I was becoming hysterical. "Do you think he had a hand in starting the fire? Patrick was here eons before Tommy, Frankie, and I ever rode our bikes up Poland Hill Road. Before we ever envisioned a life beyond what we had experienced or seen? Do you think he caused the shock I felt from the fence the others didn't?" I realized I was hyperventilating. I needed to take a breath. I needed to reach out and feel the human life around me. I understood, in a brief moment of prophetic clairvoyance, that I had left the understanding of life forgotten in an instant. My body became icy, no, frigid, in that moment of certainty.

"I think you might be on to something, Alister." Ned pulled the notes from my hand and started flipping through the pages. "Here," he threw the notebook on the table in front of me and pointed, "Here. Look at this."

I read, in Wilbur Hamilton's shakey hand, "I believe there is a door there. A door in the amusement park, under the ground maybe, I don't know where. A door that is calling all the ghosts to come to it. That clown is preventing them from going there. He has blocked the way."

I glanced up at Ned. I felt a nearly uncontrollable panic, then continued to read, "I have to go down in that cellar. I have to help them reach the park, reach the door that will lead them from this plane of existence. I have to confront that wicked, wicked clown." The words started getting bigger and more scrawled across the page. "I don't know if I can. I don't know if I can. I CAN'T DO IT!"

"Ned, what is he saying about a door? What is he talking about?"

Ned started to pace across the library floor. "I have no idea. Is that why I am here? Is that why we are all here? Is there a door we are supposed to go through?" He stopped his pacing and looked at me, his hand rubbing and rubbing that bald head. "No one has talked about a door. Oh, there have been rumors and stories about Patrick, but no one has even talked about a door that I am aware of. Why wouldn't we know?" He walked over to me and grabbed my elbow.

119

"That's it. Don't you see? Patrick is blocking us, not only from the door but from even knowing about the door. What kind of malevolent creature is he?"

I flipped through the final couple of pages in the notebook, the last words Wilbur ever wrote. "I have come to understand that I do not have it in me to go back into that cellar. I do not believe I am a coward. I believe I am not strong enough to help them. I ask all of you for forgiveness. I can not help you any more than I am able to help myself. I'm sorry."

The notes stopped. "But, he did go back down to the cellar. That's where the authorities found him. He did go back down."

Ned nodded. "Indeed he did. But he couldn't help them. It's such a pity. Well, it's up to us now, isn't it?"

"How can we help them? I don't even know where to start. Well, I know where to start. By getting rid of Pat. But I don't know how to do that. Do you?"

"No, I don't. But I need to figure it out for my own sake."

It hadn't dawned on me. Yes, for his own sake as well as all the others. I felt the panic ease from my body. "I'll help you, Ned. We'll figure something out."

Molly walked into the library. "Now, what are you two boys up to?"

Ned pulled out a chair for her at the desk, and we all sat down. We told her everything we had learned from Wilbur's notes and about the invisible wall and the door in the park.

"Isn't that a dandy?" She clucked her tongue. "What do you think about that?" She rose from the chair, "Well, all that mumbo-jumbo will wait. We have a party to get ready for?"

Ned and I glanced at each other, and I pulled out my phone and looked at the time. It was 4:00 p.m. How did that happen?

Chapter Ten

I ran out to my auto and pulled my Samsonite hard shell luggage from the boot. I only had so much in my satchel. After lugging it, thank goodness for rollers, up the five flights of stairs, I once again longed for a lift. I would have to look into that if I intended to stay here. And I did. Clown or not. It had always been my dream, as you know. I had broken quite a sweat by the time I reached my suite. After lifting it onto the bed, I opened the baggage, pulled out my best Tom Ford gray Shelton Mohair-Silk Twill pinstripe suit, and draped it over a valet chair sitting in the corner of the room. All the comforts of home. I had underestimated Mr. Wilbur Hamilton. I hung a long-sleeved white shirt in the bathroom in hopes my shower would aid in releasing it from its wrinkles.

I had missed my shampoo and body gels the past two days and placed them in the tub shower. My favorite, Jack Black's Black Reserve body and hair cleanser, infused with cardamom and cedarwood, did much to soothe my soul and ease my muddled brain. The aroma brought back the lucidity I had been missing lately.

After slipping from the shower, with a forest green towel draped around my waist, I wiped the steam from the bathroom mirror and shaved for the first time in three days. I had not realized the extent of hair growth on my cheeks and chin. Funny the things that slip the mind. I rinsed my face and blotted it with a face towel. I leaned forward toward the mirror. I did not recognize the red eyes that stared back at me, the bright blue hidden behind the scarlet. Even freshly shaved, I looked haggard. My face appeared thin.

"Brighten up, man," I said to my face in the mirror. "It won't be long 'til you see Tom and Frank." I straightened upright. "Right then."

As soon as I opened my door, voices welled up from the lobby. I peeked over the railing and saw dozens of people below dressed in a confetti of bright colors. I took the stairs down in a hurry, careful not to slip on the burgundy carpet with my shiny, spit-polished, black Oxfords. As soon as I stepped onto the lobby floor, I came to the realization that there were no live people here except me.

They swirled around me in motion, some waltzing to music that filled the room, and some just swirled in the air. Four or five feet above the ground, but all in a whirl, with me in the center. I was dizzy from the movement. They made my head spin.

"What is all this?" I asked, not sure if I should laugh or fear the spectacle around me.

Ned broke through the moving crowd and walked over to me. "They're happy. Don't you see?" He laughed and clapped me on the back. "Rumors move fast around here. They have all heard about the door in the park. It's speculation, of course, based on Wilbur's notes, but it makes sense to them. They have been awaiting your return but didn't know why. I didn't know why. But that's it. They think, I'm speculating here, that you can help us find that door. That entrance. Whatever it is."

They flew above my head in whisps of mist and smoke in many stages of form. Some were whole bodies, some were missing their legs, and upon occasion, only a head, with whisps of mist trailing behind, flew past. Those who danced had their bodies mostly intact, yet their skin sluffed down in folds, both bloodied and chared. It was an endless horrific ambiance of motion that began to unnerve me. Then, I spied a couple of the elegant partygoers from the third floor. Their golden bird masks were unmistakable. They stared directly at me, barely containing their idolatry or, worse, their hatred.

Perspiration sprouted upon my forehead and on the nape of my neck. I had undoubtedly landed myself in an actual haunt. And it was their haunt.

"I need to sit down," I said to Ned and moved toward a sofa. The very sofa I had spent the first night on. It was soft but firm, and I needed the support.

Molly approached me with a glass of champagne and what looked like a finger sandwich on a silver tray. "Here you are, Sir. A lovely bit of champagne for you. And here is a little bite to tide you over. You need a little in your stomach with the champagne." She held the tray toward me.

"Thank you, Molly. That is just what I need." I took the glass and slugged half of it down before I took the first bite of the two-bite sandwich. "Say, you told me you had invited all of my friends tonight."

"Yes, Sir. I did just that." She gestured around the lobby. "And look at them all, Sir. They are happy you are here."

Specters filled the lobby and appeared above, by the railings, looking down at me from every floor.

"But I don't know these people. Where are my friends, Tom and Frank? Where are the living people I knew when I lived in this town? Did you invite any of them?"

"Oh, these are all your friends, Sir. They all knew you when you lived in town. They all knew you would come back to them. You cared about them then, and you still do. It was a glorious day when you returned, Sir."

I think I drank a bit too much that night. I awoke on the same sofa, a blanket tucked in tightly around me.

My head throbbed. My stomach growled, and I was slightly dizzy when I rose from the couch. My suit coat hung nicely over the back of one of the wing-backed leather chairs. Thank you, Molly. My stomach growled again. I had nothing to eat since the pastry yesterday morning. There had not even been a morsel to snack on during the party. Only the endless glasses of champagne. It was no wonder Molly had not been busy preparing food for the gala. I was the only one who needed to eat. But she prepared only one tiny finger sandwich for me. I wasn't even sure what was in it. I would have to ask her about that when I saw her next.

I lifted my face and inhaled deeply. It came to my attention that I had caught a whiff of bacon in the air. The warm, greasy, and absolutely fantastic aroma of bacon. There has never been anything better for a hangover than licking a plate full of grease, in my humble opinion. I could hardly contain my glee and, forgetting my dizziness, ran for the kitchen. Elsbleth was attending to a fry skillet on the stovetop.

I halted in the doorway. Unsure of how to proceed. Elsbeth turned and waggled a two-pronged fork in my direction.

"Have a seat, Alister. I will have this right to you." She finished lifting the last dripping piece of pork onto a plate. "There is a loaf of bread in the oven and a bowl of fruit in the refrigerator. Let me get those for you."

I was surprised she called me familiar as she set the plate of bacon on the table in the center of the kitchen, and I walked hesitantly to it. My mouth, previously damp, salivating from the intense bacon aroma, turned dry, and my lips shriveled when I thought of the silver tray she held yesterday morning. The human, or so I believed, organs resting bloody upon it.

She retrieved the loaf of bread from the oven, set it on a plate, and presented it to me with a bread knife the size of Godzilla. I watched her closely as she put it on the table, unsure of what was going to happen. She smiled prettily at me and then turned to nab the fruit from the refrigerator. I sighed audibly when she also placed it on the table and then turned and left the kitchen. Whew. I don't know what I thought she might do with that knife. But the bacon again caught my attention, and I tore through the bread as if I hadn't eaten in days.

Ned walked into the room with a skip.

"Good morning, dear boy!" He said enthusiastically. He walked over, pulled a chair out from the table, and sat down beside me.

"Good morning, Ned," I mumbled quietly around my mouthful of bread. It was unlike me to talk with my mouth full. Yet I did it again, "What news from you today?"

"Oh, nothing much sport. You didn't last very long at the party. Fell asleep right on the Davenport, right in the middle of the gala, didn't you?"

"How embarrassing." I swallowed the bread, picked up my fork, then stabbed and ate a piece of an apple. "I guess I drank a bit much. I was sad Tom and Frank didn't come."

"I see. I understand that but the party was for you. They've been so excited since they heard you were buying the property."

"Yes, I must apologize to all of them at once. After breakfast." I rolled my eyes as I savored the last piece of bacon. "I would have offered it to you, Ned, but I know that wouldn't do any good."

"Oh, just the redolence makes me wish I were alive again, if for no other reason than to eat bacon." He chuckled, the sound low and rumbling deep in his throat. "Oh, and you don't need to go apologize to them. They just heard you."

"I see." I finished up and put my plate and fork in the sink. I had eaten all the bacon and fruit but found some aluminum foil to wrap around the bread. "I'm happy to know that. Now that we have the party out of the way, we need to focus on Pat. How are we going to get rid of him? Or get him out of the way or whatever we are going to do."

"That is a good question, isn't it?" Ned stood up as I walked past his chair, and we left the kitchen together.

"It's got to be in those books somewhere. The ones Wilbur stacked on the desk. If it is there, we will find it."

"Let's hit it then. I'll start on it while you go take off those suit pants. You are a bit too formal to go digging around in the cellar."

I laughed, slapped him on the shoulder, grabbed my suit coat from the chair back in front of me, and then ran up the steps. No wonder I was beginning to thin. These steps were killing me.

Ned had the books separated into three stacks when I returned. "Take a look at this one, Alister," he slid the one open in his hands across the desk to me. The book was titled *When Life Ends*. He had it marked in the middle with a piece of note paper. "Wilbur marked this spot. What do you think?"

I looked down at the book page. The chapter heading read "What Happens Now". There were pencil markings around one paragraph halfway down the page on the left.

"Ned, it talks about a door. It says, 'all beings must go through the door, an opening into the passage of the afterlife.' What do you think that means? It says it's an actual passage of the afterlife. Does that mean a passage into the afterlife? A means by which we will enter into the afterlife? Or that the afterlife is the passage of which we all have to go?"

"Well, that's just semantics, don't you think, Alister? Don't they mean almost the same thing?"

"Not exactly, Ned. If it is an actual passageway through which we must all go, maybe you, we, don't have to use it at all. Then we could be stuck here, like you and the others. But if the afterlife is the actual passageway from life, then we would all have to use it at some point, at some time, don't you think."

"I think I get you, Alister. Maybe," he shook his shiny bald head. "I'm a ghost. You'd think I would know the answer. Wouldn't you?" He crossed his arms and leaned back in his chair.

"Well, you haven't been dead very long, Ned. In the scheme of things." I flipped another page in the book but got sidetracked and set it down without thinking.

"I guess you are right there. But if Pat is guarding the actual passageway into the afterlife, he is blocking everyone from getting to their final destination. And that isn't a good thing."

"Where is your final destination, do you think, Ned?" I was curious what an actual ghost might think now that he was technically gone from life already.

"Mine? Well, Alister, I think my final destination is a beach somewhere in the South Pacific. Wouldn't that be grand?"

"It sure would be." I agreed, seeing surf and sand in my mind's eye.

"Do you think it's that easy? That Pat is blocking the door, the actual passageway to Heaven?" Ned put a new thought in my head.

"I don't know. Is that what you think, Ned?"

Ned stood up and walked to the window facing the north yard. It had begun to rain. Over his shoulder, I could see the crest and the rising top of the carousel visible in the distance. "It's either Heaven or Hell or both, I think," he answered softly.

"How could the door to Heaven and Hell be in the Poland Hill Amusement Park in Prophet, South Carolina?" I didn't expect him to answer that question. I wasn't even sure how we had arrived at it.

I sifted through the stacks of books, glancing at the titles. I slid one out of the middle. *When Life Ends*. I looked at the empty spot on the desk in front of me. We just had this book out. How did it get back into the center of the stack? I opened it back to the chapter we had looked at, "What Happens Now." The page with the paragraph we had just looked at, the paragraph about the passageway to the afterlife, was gone. Jagged edges remained. Someone had torn the page out of the book. And the following four pages. Five pages were gone.

"Ned, look at this!" I stood up as Ned turned from the window. "Someone has torn out five pages of this book. The book we just had opened. And it was in the center of the stack. Who would have done that?"

"I'll give you one guess." Ned walked back to the desk and took the book from my hands. "Well, I'll be. Guess they might have contained the information we were looking for. I guess ole' Pat didn't want us to figure anything out."

"Ned, we haven't moved. We were right here. I sure didn't see him come in. Or anyone else for that matter."

"I should have sensed him, but I didn't feel anything either. Sneaky, duplicitous fella', that one." Ned put the useless book down on top of the others. "Hey, is your phone one of those new smartphones? Can you do that internet thing and see if you can find the book and find the missing pages?"

"That's pretty forward-thinking for a ghost, Ned. But you always were one of the smartest men I have ever known." I pulled the phone from its customary place and hit the side button to wake it up. I typed in When Life Ends and received a dozen references. References regarding medical white papers, allusions to religious information, and sources touting instances of personal death scenarios filled my screen. It was easy to toss out the individual experiences about death from live people. Somewhat easy to throw out the medical explanations. No information was provided regarding the book laying in front of us.

"When was that written? I don't see it referenced anywhere here."

Ned opened the front cover of the book in question. "It says it was published in 1874 by J.B. Lippincott & Company."

I added that information to my search field with the name of the book. I instantly received information about the company. "It says they started as a bookstore in the late eighteenth century. It became J.B. Lippincott & Company, Booksellers and Stationers, in 1837. The funny thing is, while there is no mention of this book at all, the building they occupied in Philadelphia was destroyed by a fire in 1899."

"That is ironic, is it not?" Ned moved closer to my phone in an attempt to read the information for himself.

"That's about all it says. They published books on art, medicine, history, music, theology, travel, guidebooks, and novels. But there is no mention of a book titled *When Life Ends*. Nothing."

"Sounds like someone or something doesn't want us to find the book. At least those five missing pages."

"I can't believe we just had it in our hands. Why did we stop reading when we did? We must have been so close to having an answer."

"Something heinous is at work here. Don't you agree, Alister?"

I sat back down and put my phone on the desk. "Yes, I do. I have a horrific feeling about this. Does Pat have that kind of power, do you think?"

"I wouldn't think so, but there is something definitely diabolic going on here, even more diabolic than Pat." Ned sat back down. All the steam and excitement had left him. Could ghosts get dejected? He continued, "We will figure something out, Alister. You have my word on it."

Chapter Eleven

We stayed in the library until late in the afternoon. We pulled every book that dealt with death and the afterlife from the shelves. Religion, medicine, fiction, someone might be on to something, as well as fantasy, paranormal, and the occult. We pulled so many Ned had to take the occupation of a second desk. Then, lo and behold, I found a book, old, leathery, smelling of must and mold, in the back of the top shelf, left of the door. I pulled it from its dark hiding place and saw the title. *The House on Poland Hill.* Then, in my peripheral vision, I noticed the ceiling above me start to change. The white paint began to darken, bubble, and smoke over my head. A flame leaped through and flashed before my face. I nearly fell off the ladder. I lost control of the book. It flew out of my grasp and landed neatly on the desk in front of Ned.

"What's this?" Ned had leaped from his chair as it struck in front of him. He looked up at me on the ladder but made no notice of the inflamed ceiling overhead.

Could spirits get injured by falling objects, I wondered. "Good God, Ned, look at the title of that book." I stepped down the ladder as swiftly as I was able, keeping an eye out for falling flames. "I didn't know such a book existed. Most of everything I knew about this place came from newspaper and magazine articles. Or the courthouse, surveyor's office, that kind of thing. Why didn't I know there was an actual book about it?" I walked over to Ned and the book, "Come to think of it, why would I have believed no one ever wrote a book about it? After all, Truline Atherton had died here. Dozens had died from the fire." I picked the book up and flipped it over in my hand to glance at the back. "I should have known there was a book." I looked back at Ned, then up at the still-smoking ceiling, "Shouldn't I have?"

"Now, Alister, remember, I have been in this town all of my life, and I never knew anyone ever wrote a book. You were only twelve when you left to go back to England. I was amazed your dad did as much as he did to help you research this place. It was your vision, after all, not his, that sparked your desire to study this place."

"It wasn't a vision nor a desire, Ned. It has been much more than that. I fear this mansion has put its clutches deep into my very soul. No wonder all the spirits here know me. They could feel me as much as I could and did feel them. Spooky, isn't it?"

"I'll tell you again for all of us. We are mighty glad you are here, Alister."

"Well, I am happy to oblige." Holding the book in my left hand, I reached over and patted his shoulder with my right one.

I turned and pulled the chair from my appointed desk and moved it over to his. We sat down together and opened the book before us. The copyright page said the book was written and published in 1944.

Ten years after the fire swept the hillside. Wilbur Hamilton must have found it prior to, or during, his residence and hidden it on that shelf.

"Why do you think he hid it?" I asked aloud, more out of curiosity than the need to know.

"You got me, pal."

"Look here. It has everything in it, from the time the spas and park were built to the additions of the main house and the pool house. There is a chapter about Ms. Atherton and then the fire. Wait, what's this? Chapter six has a list with the names of everyone who ever stayed in the hotel." I had a thought. I wasn't sure I wanted to look, but I flipped to the last page of the chapter, to the very bottom of that list. And there they were, the final two entries on the page. The number 785. The name Ned Abernathy had been written beside the number. Below that was the number 786 and the name Alister Prescott.

My body froze. An icy path of fear spread from my toes to the top of my brain. My entire body felt suddenly filled with frozen tin. An acrid, metallic scent hit my nostrils, and the taste of tin exploded in my mouth. The taste of fear. The book sat on the desk, silent and dark. But my name on that page screamed at me. I couldn't move. My name was the very last name on that page. Did the story of this house end with me? Is that what I was seeing? My breath caught in my chest, and I wondered if I was going to suffocate right here in this room, right now, without another chance to find out what was really going on here.

"Well, that's a pip."

Ned's nonchalance expression loosened my chest. The air exploded from my lungs, transported on the waves of my hysterical laugh. Tears sprung from my eyes and slid down my cheeks.

Ned looked at me with a casualness I certainly did not feel. His composure spoke of an ability I did not possess. I knew it wasn't indifference to my role in all of this, to our names written on that page, but his comfort with the inviolate situation he now found himself in.

My laughter and tears subsided as I stared into those eyes. The eyes of my long-lost but suddenly found mentor. I nodded at him, feeling comfort there, "Yes, Ned. That's a pip."

Ned pulled the book closer to himself and flipped through the pages. "Did you see anything about Patrick Monaghan in here?"

I composed myself, "Oh, we should look for him. See what it says about him, if anything." I agreed and patiently waited while he looked for something, anything.

At last, he said, "Nothing. I don't see a thing about him."

I don't know why I didn't think of it before, "Who is the author, Ned?"

Ned flipped back to the copyright page. "Randolph N. Whitney Jr."
He looked back at me. "Son of the original hotel owner, Randolph
Noble Whitney."

"Mr. Whitney died in the hotel fire," I said. "The newspaper said he
had taken time off from his duties and was in the pub, having a drink,
when the fire started. It started right under the pub. Something with
the coal burner down in the cellar. I don't think they ever figured it
out, exactly. There was a stampede of patrons. Knocked him down
and ran him over on the way to the doors. Broke a leg and couldn't
get himself out with the lot of them. His wife died up in room 515."
Why hadn't I thought of that? My memory hadn't worked correctly
since entering this establishment just a few days ago. "The very room
I am staying in now. I hadn't realized that until now."

"What about Junior? How did he get out?"

"He was at school that day. It was a Friday. The park was open and
ready for the upcoming holiday. He hadn't been let out of school yet.
Schools closed at noon that day. Memorial Day weekend it was. They
called it Decoration Day back then, of course. Didn't change it to
Memorial Day until 1971."

"Oh, I knew that. I forgot."

"The park was already packed when the fire started. It couldn't
have been worse timing. Mr. Whitney was probably having a nip
before the weekend really got started. I'm sure he was going to get

pretty busy with all those guests." I suddenly felt sorry for the chap. He lost his wife, his hotel, and his life having that last wee dram. "So Junior doesn't mention Patrick Monaghan? He was here then, wasn't he."

"Indeed, he was." Ned rubbed his bald head.

I was beginning to think it was a nervous quality he gained after losing his hair. He still had it when I knew him those years ago.

"I wonder if Junior ever had a run-in with him? That would be something a young fellow would never forget. And something he would write about."

"Yes, he would." Ned returned to the pages before him. He scanned at an incredible speed, turning one page after another.

I guess spirits pick up the nack of reading at a faster speed than we live beings. Although, I thought I could read pretty fast.

At last, he stopped short of the end of the book. Just a page or two away from the last one. He sat back hard in his chair and looked up at me. He reached up to push up his glasses, which were absent from his face. Ghosts don't need glasses.

"Well, I'll be damned." He said.

"What did you find?"

"He did see him. He was down in that cellar." He turned back one page, "He says his dad had him go down to look for an oil can."

"Holy shit, I saw that oil can. Pat had it in his hand."

139

"Whitney needed to help get the coal furnace going again. It had gone out during a nasty storm. Had three guys down there trying to get it started again. Randolph Junior went down into that cellar by himself. He says he was about to reach for the oil can when a chubby, pink-cheeked fellow reached out and took it from him."

"That's just what happened to me, Ned."

"Junior was so startled he started to cry. He says the man patted him on the top of his head and then handed him the oil can. And when Junior turned to leave the cellar, he glanced over his shoulder to say goodbye to the kind, strange man and was confronted by a friendly clown. The clown smiled at him, patted him on the shoulder, and waved goodbye. He says he never went into the cellar again. Yet, when penning the book, felt the need to include the nice clown in the pages."

"Well, that doesn't sound like the same Patrick The Clown to me."

"Oh, but it does, don't you see? Pat The Clown was a real clown. He had to love children. Something had to have happened to him. Something so sinister that he changed. Something," Ned tapped his finger on the book, thinking.

"But the park was full of adults and children when the fire swept through. There should be lots of children's spirits here. Shouldn't there be? I have only seen one. It was an infant, but it was dead. Really dead." Did that mean the infant didn't have a spirit or a soul

140

when he was alive? I didn't understand. I couldn't remember seeing any young apparitions since I had arrived. The youngest one I could recall was a boy about seventeen years old. My thoughts were scattered, but my mouth said clearly, "Where are all the children, Ned?"

Ned looked stupefied. "Why, I don't know, Alister. I guess I hadn't even noticed these six years. I was a school teacher, Alister. How could I not miss the children?"

I turned and looked out the windows at the darkening sky. The drapes that hung on each side of the widows had caught on fire, and I could feel the heat against my cheeks. I turned and looked over my shoulder at Ned. I said, "Ned, what has Pat done with the children?"

Chapter Twelve

That was the decision maker. We looked at each other like we had just found a huge missing piece of the puzzle. If this was a puzzle. If not, what was it? We went to the kitchen in search of Molly. She was in the Butler's pantry pulling packages of lollypops open.

"I knew you were coming. You are right. Something here has been keeping us from missing the children. Why would someone do such a thing?"

Ned turned to me, "How many children died in the fire?"

"I don't know. I never saw a division in numbers between adults and kids in anything I read. And if there are adults here from times past, wouldn't there also be children here from other times as well? Not just the ones who died here in the fire?"

"Good question," Molly handed us the bags full of lollypops. "If we are going to find them, these might help." She shrugged. "I know we can't taste anything. I don't know about the children. They might find comfort even if they can't taste them."

I grabbed the bag. "Thanks, Molly. I sure hope it helps. Why do you think the parents haven't asked about their children?"

She stood with her hands wringing her apron, "Maybe they didn't know they were missing like we didn't. Best of luck to you both. I hope you find them. For all our sakes."

Ned and I grabbed the torches from the pantry that we had used to look out the mystic kitchen door at the cave. The door, I suddenly realized, Molly didn't stray far from with the exception of the lobby and the library. Wonder who made up the beds, then? Elsbeth?

"Where will we start, Ned? I would think the kids might come out with Molly sacking the lollies, but they didn't. Where do you think they are?" My mind was a twisted molten magma of thought. Questions, possibilities, and ideas swirled faster and faster, and I could feel that treacherous taste of frozen tin filling me again. My throat and chest began to tighten.

"In my opinion, if ole' Pat is keeping us from going to the amusement park, that's where they are."

"But Wilbur's notes and the book said there is a passageway there. Why would he keep the kids there? Couldn't they use the passage?"

"Because he loves the kids and wants them near him. That's what I think. And, sometimes, children don't know what they are supposed to do without advice. Maybe Pat is the only one who gives them advice. What then?"

"I guess the cellar is the best place to start looking then." That metal feeling moved into my head. My brain hurt.

We ran through the kitchen center directly to that hallway, the one without the windows, the one I had found myself in only three days ago.

"I haven't seen this hallway before."

"It isn't in the building plans either," I answered. "Just like the wall for the tavern. The wall should, in all rights, go out over the south parking lot and into the lawn if the scale were correct. Question Ned. The lollies might lure the children, but what are we going to do to lure Pat away so we can get to the children?"

I had no answer. The hall was brilliantly white, and the wall lamps exaggerated the light where windows should have been.

"How far is the cellar?"

I noticed Ned no longer ran on human legs but had lost solidity below the waist. I ran to keep up with him. "We go as far as the hallway goes. It seems like it took me forever to walk there and back. I think time might be a little variable here."

When time is off, isn't it funny how it shifts? Sometimes turning back in and folding upon itself? Something that might have happened before happens again. Like a deranged déjà vu. We have all heard it since time was discovered. That it might change, could change in the blink of an eye. And not just time. Space. Wormholes. Hadn't I learned in university that space can fold unto itself, and one might enter in one plane and come out into another? Well, that's what happened to Ned and me as we ran down that hallway. The hallway had only led into that cellar room with the clown. That wasn't what happened this time.

We walked for a few minutes more and came to the first curve I witnessed the first time. Ned stopped suddenly and looked back over his shoulder. I looked back to see what he was looking at. We weren't alone. I jumped back about a foot when I solidly hit a specter who had stopped right behind me. One gray eye popped from his left socket, and he reached up to put it back in place. He grinned at me with a face that no longer had lips. His nose was missing, and other than those gray eyes, charred teeth made up most of his face. About a dozen spirits accompanied him. They followed in varied degrees of corporality. Those in more human form, solid with burned and rotting flesh, were the nearest. The whiffs of mist, smoke, and ectoplasm stayed to the rear of the crowd. I was speechless.

"Hello, men," Ned spouted. "Thank you for joining us." He turned to me and slapped me on the shoulder. "It's wonderful to have good help." We continued around the curve, and then Ned said, "I thought you said it went straight to the cellar." Ned slowed his flight as we approached a fork in the hall in front of us. The hall didn't just split off in one other direction. It split off into two.

"Wow, this is new." I stopped short, and the bag of lollies slapped my hip where I had tied it to my belt. "There was only one hallway the last time I was here. It led straight to Pat. It went northwest from the kitchen and then curved straight north. None of these halls look like they go north."

I ran a few feet down the passage to my left with three souls hot on my heels behind me. The hall turned and headed east. It would lead under the old beauty salon and past the tower, out to where the race track used to be. We returned to the fork. Ned was getting back from his excursion with his posse after checking out the passage to the far right.

"It doubles back and goes toward the kitchen. I went the entire length. It comes out from underground. A ladder sits at the end of the passage under what looks like a trap door. I speculate it might come out somewhere in that cave." He floated just above the ground in front of me. "It's a real shame."

"What's a real shame."

"If that trap door was there when Molly was. They could have used it to escape that place." He hung his head and shook it sadly. "They might have had a chance after all."

"I doubt if it was there then, Ned," I tried to console him. "It wasn't even there on Friday."

"Oh, right!" He looked at me and smiled. "Thanks, Alister."

I think it made him feel a bit better. I began to realize he might have a thing for Molly. I think it made a kind of logic.

"I guess we take the hall in the center. By all accounts, it should lead to the garden room in the cellar and the door that blocks us. It may have only moved a bit." I started in that direction, and Ned followed without saying a word.

We walked for what seemed like ten minutes. Again, an extraordinary amount of time that should have taken us over the crest of the hill. And it did. We did not find the end of the hallway leading to the garden room. We did find a door at the end of the hallway. Ned and I took that door. It exited under the open sky, thirty feet or so, under the crest of the north ridge. The other ghosts did not go out with us. They stayed inside, with looks of longing on their tattered faces, and closed the door behind us.

"What's that all about?" I asked Ned. I thought they wanted to help us." Ned only shrugged.

I turned and looked behind me, up at the house above us. The tower spire was all I could see over the tops of the dense trees and foliage covering the space between us. I returned my gaze to look out over the hill where we found ourselves. The top of the carousel was now more exposed than it had been from the manse above.

There was a footpath at our feet, leading from the door. We followed the pathway, weaving around some of the most beautiful Southern Live Oaks I had ever seen. Giant beautiful trees, sunlit leaves showing brightly green. Their branches twisted and intertwined, constructing a live barrier we had to climb through to make our way.

We didn't know where the footpath would lead us. But as the trees moved, grew, and twisted in front of our eyes, it was evident we were being led.

Ned laughed out loud. "This is stupendous!" He clapped his hands with joy. "That darn invisible barrier has kept me on top of the hill since I got here six years ago! What glorious miracle is this?" He flew in and out through the interwoven lace of branches as though he had already found the amusement park.

The sun shone high in the sky, making it appear to be early afternoon. But it wasn't. We had left the library as the sun was setting in the west. But it was full daylight. But what day? I pulled my phone out of my pocket for a quick look at the time and date. I had no signal.

"Isn't that interesting?"

Ned flew and hovered in front of me. "What is?"

"I have no signal," I answered and slid the useless phone back where it came from. "We left the library after it was starting to get dark." I looked up above the tree line, "now look at it. It's broad daylight. I find that extremely interesting."

"I wish I could breathe in the fresh air. I wish I could get a lung full of the fragrance of green of the leaves, the grass, and flowers. Look at the towering Palmetto trees. Beautiful!"

"Ned, what grass and flowers?" I looked suddenly around me. There were wildflowers. And Wisteria. Beautiful purple clusters hung down from the trees. And Goldenrod was scattered everywhere. I looked beside my feet as Goldenrod sprouted up instantly around me and grew incredibly fast to reach my shoulders in a flash. I looked at Ned and laughed. "You are right, this is incredible! How are they growing so fast? Why are they here? It's late September!"

"Alister, I don't ever want to go back into that rubble. I'm tired of seeing charred furniture soot everywhere. Look at this beautiful landscaping. Why, I don't even see any of the trees retaining a bit of evidence that they had been in a fire."

"Wait, Ned," I was taken aback. "What do you mean you don't want to go back to the rubble? Charred furniture? I don't know what you are talking about."

"The fire, Alister. The state of the house. You know Wilbur Hamilton only restored the one guest suite for himself. I don't know how he lived there all those years with it that way. It's a wonder it wasn't required to be torn down after the fire. The damage was so profound. But he moved into it anyway." He dropped to his feet, which suddenly appeared below him. He stared at me for a brief moment and then said, "Come to think of it, I don't know how you were able to purchase it in its current shape either."

I was stunned. "I don't know what you are talking about, Ned. Hamilton restored the entire house. Why, every detail, down to the scrollwork on the hotel concierge desk, is exquisite. Mrs. Wintergreen said it only needed some minor repair, and she was right, wasn't she?"

"Alister, just look at the flowers!" He laughed and took off into the air.

"You're a bloody fool," I screamed at the sky. "Confounded idiot! Come back here."

I pulled my legs from the encroaching wildflowers and ran down the footpath in the direction Ned had flown. He had made me angry. I had no idea what he was talking about. But as I leaped over and under tree boughs, with the fragrance of wildflowers in my nose and the song of birds trilling in the air, I began to mellow. All thoughts of Ned's comments about the house left me without another thought. I followed the footpath to where it led me, around to the northeast side of the hill.

"Ned," I scanned the sky and the trees and spun my body in circles, looking for him. "Where did you go, mate? I can't see you. Come on back, buddy."

As I spun, it dawned on me that I saw a building flash by, and I stopped mid-turn. Squinting my sun-blinded eyes, I could make out the solid concrete form.

"What's this?" I asked myself. "Who put this here?" No one answered me. "Well, let's just have a look, shall we?" And just like that, I started talking to myself.

I skipped down the pathway that led directly to the building's door. I skipped. I haven't skipped since I was probably six years old. The building was concrete. Massive in length and rectangular. The door was sealed tightly shut and bolstered by a large metal padlock, like the one that chained the front gate that day that Tommy, Frankie, and I had tried to get in. Tommy and Frankie. I had forgotten all about them. Weren't they supposed to have come to visit over the weekend? But, the weekend was gone. It was Monday. Wasn't it?

I picked up the padlock, and rust flaked and crumbled over my palm.

"Alister, you are an incredible mix of British and American. You use words like flashlight and torch simultaneously. What did you find?"

I startled and dropped the padlock with a clunk. "Ned, where did you go?" But I laughed out loud. "That is a fine trick indeed. You need to teach me how to do that! Where were you?"

"Oh, just here and there. Taking in the sites. What do you have here?"

"It's a building, Ned. Concrete. Has a lock on the outside of the door. And yes, I know I am. I was in the U.S. from age seven to twelve. My language formative years, you know, and I don't know what this is. Do you want to find out?" I said eagerly.

"Sure, Alister. What else do we have to do?"

"Right, that!" But something nagged at the corner of my mind. I didn't know there was something I needed to remember.

Grabbing the padlock, I gave it a sharp twist, and it fell apart in my hand.

"That was easy," Ned said, hovering over my shoulder.

"Let's go see what is inside. Do you still have your flashlight?"

"I do indeed." He alighted to his feet.

We stepped into immediate darkness.

"Another hallway," I said. "I'm really getting tired of hallways."

"Where does it lead, Alister?"

"Well, I don't know, Ned." I flipped on my torch.

The hallway was short. I was thankful for that. It led to a room large enough to echo when I took a step. Ned made no sound. We shone our lights around the ample space and tried to get our bearings and determine where we were. My torch flashed across a door with a sign. It read Electrical Room. Good fortune, indeed. I slipped in without alerting Ned. After leaving the door open, I flipped the switches in the breaker box. The entire building lit up.

"Way to go, Alister!" Ned called from outside the door. "Wow, you have got to see this!"

I hurried out to see what Ned was exclaiming about. The place was huge. It housed one gigantic, rectangular room with several smaller rooms around the perimeter of the outer wall. All of the rooms had signs above the doors, just like the Electricle Room. Men's Changing Room, Women's Changing Room, Sauna, Hot Tubs, Lockers. The center of the not one, but three Olympic-sized swimming pools.

"Well, what do you think of that?" I voiced aloud. "I knew this place had a pool. I didn't know they had three like this!"

I stepped to the side of the pool that was closest to me and looked down. It was full of water. Fresh, clear, sparkling water. I bent down and felt it with my fingers. Cool, refreshing. I wanted to strip off my clothes and go for a swim. I started to lift my shirtwaist when Ned caught my attention.

"I wouldn't do that, Alister." He beckoned to me, "Come, look over here."

I hurried over to the pool where Ned was standing. The third one. Sunlight flickered through a window in the back door near the pool as I approached Ned, and it flashed brightly in my eyes. I couldn't see anything until a bluish fog moved in front of me. I almost stepped off the side of the pool. Ned caught hold of my arm and stopped my plunge. I stepped out of the direct sunlight and looked into the pool where Ned was pointing. My breath caught in my chest, and I couldn't speak for a moment.

The pool was full of bodies. Dead ones. Hundreds piled on top of one another, stacked up to the rim of the pool. There were no spirits here. I realized Ned still had ahold of my arm, holding it with a tight

153

grasp I would not have thought possible for a specter of any kind. We stood there, staring, engrossed in the macabre, unsure of what to do or say. I looked back at the other two pools. They still appeared to be filled with only fresh, clear water. Water to soothe and cool my soul within its refreshing embrace. If I could but slide down the side into one of those pools. Ah, what a release I might find. A release that I suddenly yearned for above all else. A sweet, sweet release of all the anxiety that had controlled me for the last few days. But instead, I turned my head back to the horror before me. And right there, in front of our eyes, the bodies began to move. Several rocked back and forth, attempting to turn over. And we stood there, Ned and I, frozen in front of what looked like the ravages from a massacre. We watched as arms began to poke up out of the mass of corpses. Arms searching for purchase on the pool side walls. Pulling and moving and pushing, and then heads, heads began to pop up from where the arms had previously reached. Searching, eyes bulged out, trying to find purchase through a solid handhold from which to rise and leave this freakish mound of flesh.

The entire Olympic-sized pool began to undulate with corpses of rotting flesh. It was a singular body of grotesque fluidity. A hideous mixture of popping joints and squishing, liquid sounds. My mind could not understand the scene my eyes saw happening in front of me. Oh, yes, I had become accustomed to the ghost, the specter, even the fire burnt flesh of the revenants of the Poland Hill fire, but this, this was something altogether different. This was a living, moving pool of decomposing flesh. Only one word flared within my horrified mind. Zombies. There were Zombies here. I realized in that horrific moment that, like Wilbur Hamilton, I was in way over my head. I could not do it. I could not help them. Any of them.

I looked at Ned. I wanted to whisper to him that I was done. I was finished. I started to whimper, thinking that I had to leave at once, but at that very moment, something grabbed my ankle. And as I looked down at the zombie arm of bones attached to the hand that encircled my ankle, I screamed. Oh, yes, I screamed. I screamed louder and more insane than I had ever heard anyone scream. I could not look at Ned. I wrested my leg free from that nefarious grasp and ran. I ran without a care for anyone else in this world. I ran out of the pool house and through the cops of trees that lined the path back toward the house up on Poland Hill. Crazed beyond my own mind's wildish beliefs and beyond.

I awoke and found myself flung upon a low-hanging branch of a Southern Live Oak covered in Spanish Moss. Mist had arisen and covered me in an extraordinary layer of drizzle. It did much to cool my wits. I sat up, glanced around, and tried to determine where I was. The memories of Ned's and my last hours were gone. I couldn't remember why we were outside of the hotel. But in my foggy

155

memory, I knew I was missing Ned. I scanned the hill around me but could see no glimpse of him anywhere.

It flooded back in the next second. I remembered the pool room. How could I have forgotten something so twisted? I shivered at the remembrance of the grip of bones around my ankle and shuddered. I leaned over and threw up on the dirt path.

"Well, that is a fine good morning to you!" Ned appeared out of thin air and sat down on the branch beside me.

"Oh, man, Ned. Did you see that? Did you see those zombies?" I wanted to vomit again. This was becoming a serious habit of late.

"Wow, Alister," he said, "I had no idea zombies really existed."

I caught his eye and raised an eyebrow. "Ned, really?"

"Okay, Okay," he chuckled. "I guess if I can believe that I, myself, am a ghost, I should believe in zombies. Is that what you think?"

"Well, something like that anyway." I patted the back of his hand that rested upon his knee. "It's good to see you, mate."

"And good to see you too, Alister." Ned agreed.

"I think I am ready to head back to the house. Yeah? I need to regroup before we try to find the amusement park. After what we just saw, I don't think I'm ready to confront Pat yet." I stood up and started to walk up the path to the house. "I need a really stiff drink."

Ned and I followed the path back toward the house, but it led us directly into a side of shale rock on the face of the ridge. There was no door in which to enter the hallway under the hill.

"Well, what do you think about that?" Ned pushed his hands against the rock wall to no avail. "Where did the door go?"

I looked up and saw that haunting tower spire rising over the crest of the hill. "Guess we have to find a way up the side." It was not what I wanted to do. I was exhausted, both physically and mentally, and was ready to stop and drop right where I stood. I looked to the west and saw the road which led from the house to the theme park. It wasn't too far away. "Let's go," I stepped off the path and trudged through the knee-high golden rods and around outcroppings of rock until I reached the road. The strain that tugged at the backs of my tired thighs and calfs attempted to deter me as I climbed that rugged driveway to the top. As I climbed, with Ned hovering ever at my shoulder, I realized that the sun had given way to the darkness of the actual hour. I slipped the mobile from my pocket, and it showed 10:45 p.m. on its face. I had not missed Monday night after all.

I came to the place where Ned and I had raced to just earlier in the day and stopped short. I didn't know what we were going to do to get around the solid, invisible wall before me. I turned around to rest my back against it to think and fell right onto the ground with a thump, my back hitting a puddle in the gravel of the drive as the drizzle fell from the dark sky.

"Well, this place sure keeps us hopping," Ned flew past me across the plane where the wall had been.

"Yeah, great." I rolled to my knees, rose to my feet, and lifted my face into the cool drizzle and breeze of the night sky."

Chapter Thirteen

I followed Ned to the side of the mansion to the outside door of The Prancing Pony. My body begged for rest as I pulled open the heavy door and dragged myself into the pub.

"What'll it be, Mr. Prescott, Sir?" Charles asked as he wiped the bar top to a shine in front of where I stood, then turned to slip a bottle back onto the shelf behind him.

I planted myself on a pub stool at the bar with relief. Something was comforting in the way he was constantly polishing the bar top or a glass. "A bourbon, please, Mr. Reese," I answered and looked beside me for Ned. He wasn't there. Tonight, there were but a handful of specters lurking around the pub.

"Sure thing, Sir." Charles put a glass in front of me on the bar and poured it full.

I picked it up and slammed it down in one swig. "Another," I said.

"Of course, Sir." Charles filled it full a second time.

After pouring it down my throat as quickly as the first, I looked again at Charles. "One more, please?" I was starting to calm down a bit.

"No need to ask, Sir," he said as he filled my glass a third time.

This time, I took a nice long sip but set it on the counter three-fourths full. "Thank you, Charles."

"Of course, Sir." He pulled a bar towel from the counter in front of me and wiped up a few dribbles I had sloshed there. The bar was again shiny and pristine. It needed no more wiping. "If you don't mind my asking, have you had a bad day, Sir," Charles inquired.

"No, no, Charles," I glanced around the pub, "I don't mind you asking, but didn't I see this pub on fire the other day?"

"I don't know what you are talking about, Sir." He set the towel aside. "This place is precisely the same as when you were in the other night, Sir."

"Yes, quite," I replied. "Of course it is."

"Will you be having another, Sir?"

I looked down at the glass in my hand, and it was empty again. "No, thank you, Charles. I think that will do it for tonight." I looked back up at him and at the flames that had suddenly appeared behind him, lapping at the scrolled wood around the bar mirror.

"Yes, Sir. Anytime, Sir." Charles answered with a smile.

I rose from the barstool and rubbed both hands through my hair. I nodded at Charles and left the pub through the door that entered the lobby. My lobby. My new home. I looked back over my shoulder at Charles. His hair was on fire.

The lobby was lit up for the night. The lamps and wall sconces brightly glowed. There were no ghosts in attendance this evening. I didn't hear a sound except for my shoes tapping against the marble floor. I took the north staircase to the fifth floor. Welcomed the roaring fire in the hearth to wipe the chill of the night drizzle from my still-damp skin and crawled into bed without another thought.

I awoke on Tuesday morning feeling every single ache in my muscles and bones. Someone had attended the fireplace while I slept as the flames still leaped up the flue. Somehow, the thought of someone entering my room while I slept did not worry me. It had to be Molly. Right? I grabbed a fresh blanket from the bedroom closet and walked out into the glass den Wilbur Hamilton had built off the bedroom, the one that looked out over the south lawn. The sky was dark, the clouds swollen with rain. I pulled the blanket around my shoulders and settled down in the overstuffed armchair.

I wished I had a big mug of steep coffee when the bedroom door opened, and Molly swirled in. She waltzed into the den and placed a steaming hot mug on the table beside me.

"I thought you might need a nice cup of steep coffee this morning, Mr. Prescott." She winked at me. It seemed all worry from the night before about the missing children had left her mind.

"Thank you, Molly." I realized the other day I thought Elsbeth was the one who readied my room, but it must have been Molly after all. It tasted better than any cup of joe I had enjoyed in my entire life. I held the steam beneath my nose and inhaled deeply. Snuggled deep inside the blanket, inside the fire-heated room, and with the warmth of the mug within my hand, I felt the most comfortable I had ever felt in this house. I might never move from this moment or space in time.

Molly had slipped out unannounced, and I sat for quite some while, listening to the rain patter on the glass around me.

I suddenly heard a tap, tap, tap and looked up from my mug to the window. Outside, on the window sill, sat a blackbird. It was not big enough to be a raven, no, but I recognized it as a Great-tailed grackle. I had seen many in flocks around town as a child. He perched upon the sill, rain falling onto his iridescent black and purple feathers, and stared at me with his bright yellow eyes. I stared back at him as he reached forward and tapped the window again. He shivered and flicked his broad, long tail to rid it of the rain. But his bright yellow eyes never left my bright blue ones. He was a crow but a fine specimen, long and slim. He raised his beak into the air as if to catch a drop of rain, and at once, I felt he was a kindred spirit. I felt as if I were looking at myself in a mirror. He pecked at that glass window as if to urge me to rise and let him inside. I resisted the urge and watched him closely. I decided right then and there to name him Percy. Percy and I were the same. I could feel it in his eyes.

"Good morning, Percy, my fine fellow." I smiled at him, and I swear he smiled back.

I think I dozed there. For when I awoke, the empty coffee mug sat on the side table, and Percy was gone. The rain continued to pelt upon the glass around me, but I realized it had turned to ice. Little ice pellets began to stack upon one another and stack and stack, and as I watched, the ice grew to over an inch thick. I'm not sure how long I sat there, watching the ice build, when I felt a tap upon my shoulder. I jumped and threw the blanket from my shoulders, rose, and spun to look behind me in one swift movement.

"What are you doing here?" Ned asked me.

"Good God, Ned," I held my hand to my chest, "You nearly frightened me to death."

"I ask again, Alister, what are you doing here?"

"Why, I don't know what you mean, Ned?" I really didn't know what he meant.

"I have been waiting for you all day." He walked back into the bedroom, and I followed along behind him.

I noticed the fire in the hearth was out, and the room had taken a chill. "The fire went out," I said, nonplussed. "Why did Molly let that happen?"

"Molly, what in blazes are you going on about? Molly has been helping me look for you all day. Where have you been?"

"What do you mean, where have I been?" I wasn't sure where this conversation was leading. "I woke up this morning and have been sitting here, in the den, talking to Percy. Molly brought me a cup of coffee this morning, and I guess I wasn't ready to start functioning yet to figure out what we needed to do today."

"What to do today? You know what we needed to work on today." He paced back and forth across the room. "You know we have to figure out what to do about that damn clown. We have to find out where he has the kids. Molly has been with me since this morning, looking for you. She didn't bring you any cup of coffee. I looked here in your suite for you. You were not here." He reached out and smacked me with a sharp slap to the face. "And who the hell is Percy?"

"What?"

He stopped pacing in front of me, "Alister, it's 7:00 p.m., and we have done nothing today. And what den are you talking about?"

I awoke then from the daze I hadn't been aware I was in and spun around the bedroom as I came out of the dreamlike state. Where the den had been, where I had been sitting all day, was a solid wall. No window was even installed within. I ran to the wall and ran my hand across it. I couldn't believe my eyes. I turned and ran back and stared at the painting of the old hotel that hung on the chimney wall. No glass room was painted there.

"What's this?" I looked wild-eyed at Ned.

He didn't have a suitable response. "I don't know what you are talking about, Alister. But let's go down to the kitchen and get you something to eat. You don't look so good." He removed the thick blanket that had remained about my shoulders. I wore only my skivvies and a pair of socks. "Well, you best get dressed first, I think. I'm not sure what Molly would think seeing you in this state." He went to my dresser and pulled out a pair of blue jeans and a long-sleeved light blue tee shirt.

"Sure, Ned." I gazed blankly at him, "That sounds good." I sat down on the bed and pulled on the jeans and shirt he had handed me.

He opened the closet door in the north wall and pulled out a pair of sturdy, leather hiking boots. "I think these should do. I'm not sure where we will end up this evening." He said with a bit of unearthly hollowness in his voice. He helped me slip them on over my socks and tied them tightly for me. He stood back up and looked at me, "I guess that will have to do. Let's get a move on it. Molly has had dinner ready for some time." He turned toward the door to the hallway.

I pulled myself up from the bed and turned one more time to look behind me before following Ned out of the room. There was still just a solid wall where I had spent an apparent entire day. We took the stairs down those damn five flights and went straight to the kitchen. Molly met us right at the kitchen table with a pot of stew. It smelled absolutely divine. I realized Ned was right. I hadn't eaten anything all day. Was he right about the coffee, too? I was sure Molly had brought the steaming mug to me this morning. But how could she have if the room wasn't really even there?

I felt my legs shake as I lowered myself onto the kitchen chair. "Molly, that smells fantastic." I picked up the spoon and shoveled the beef and vegetables into my mouth as fast as I could. I ignored the heat as it slid down my throat. "So good," I mumbled and tore off a piece of bread from the loaf beside me. It followed the stew with hardly a chew.

"Slow down, Mr. Prescott. I don't want you to choke yourself," she gasped.

I finally emptied my mouth enough to say, "Thank you, Molly. I didn't realize how hungry I was."

Ned had watched me plow through the food with hardly a breath, "Are you good now, Alister?" He asked honestly.

I wiped my mouth with a napkin and smiled. "Yes, I'm good, Ned." I rose from my seat. "Let's go get this figured out. Thanks again, Molly. You are the best!"

"Why," she blushed, "thank you, Alister. Always a pleasure," and reached over and grabbed my plate from the table.

Ned and I took our daily walk back to the library. It was now 8:00 on Tuesday night. I first met our menace, Patrick Monaghan, on Friday night. It had taken this long to figure out who he was, and we had yet to figure out what to do about him.

We had found absolutely nothing either in the library books or in Wilbur Hamilton's wondering notes to help us to date.

"I don't know what we are looking for," I said to Ned. "But for some reason, I feel like we are running out of time."

"I get that same feeling," Ned agreed. "I think I am getting that feeling because of the children."

"Me too!" I agreed wholeheartedly. "I know that Patrick has been here since before the hotel was built, so there are a lot of children he has been collecting for some time. But I totally agree with you. I also feel that time is growing short if we are to help them. And to help you and the others." I skimmed through all the books we had pulled from the library shelves. "What to do, What to do?" I murmured under my breath.

"He scared you. That's what you told me. That's what Wilbur wrote in his notebook. But if you remember reading *The House on Poland Hill*, that Randolph Whitney kid wasn't scared. He said the clown was nice to him. Said he gave him the oil can to help his dad."

"Yes, Ned. To help his dad burn down the hotel. If you recall, that oil can helped cause the hotel fire." I stopped for a moment, and then a thought came to me. It had to be, "Ned, what if there wasn't oil in that can? What if Pat had put something explosive in it?" I grew agitated now, "Could that be it?"

167

"But the book said the kid got the oil can for his dad. The fire didn't start until the next day when Junior was at school, right?"

"That's right. But the papers said that an explosion in the boiler room caused the fire. Those furnaces ran on coal, with oil. There would be nothing there to cause an explosion unless something else was in that can. And what if the furnace men tried to continue to light it that day without the oil can? What if Randolf Sr. didn't give it to them until the next morning for some reason?"

"That is an excellent deduction, Ali. I should have thought of that." Ned flipped through the Poland Hill book. "I have an idea. Why don't we go and see if we can find Pat? Call him out with our thoughts on the matter. If he loved children as much as we think, and he was the one who gave Junior the accelerant to start that fire or have his dad start it, maybe we can play on the fact that all the children died because of him. Maybe he knows that already. But maybe he didn't know what was in that can, gave it to the kid, and has been regretting it ever since."

"That's a pretty big leap, Ned." I shook my head. "But, I guess it is worth a try."

"Well, let's see if we can find that cellar and see about that."

That same feeling of spontaneous fear hit me like a truck, but I said, "Ok. Let's go talk to him." I had another thought, "Ned, if the oil can caused the explosion that started the fire, how did it get back into the cellar?"

Ned shrugged but said nothing.

I pulled myself from the chair and wondered if I had gone insane.

Chapter Fourteen

With flashlights/torches in hand, Ned and I went straight back to the hallway leading north from the rear of the kitchen. This time, there were no strange hallways leading out in multiple directions. This time, it led straight to the verticle drop, and this time, steps appeared right in front of our eyes, and we stepped down onto the cellar floor. The last time I was here, the thought of looking for a light switch was beyond my mind's capability. This time, I shone the torch around the room and spotted a wall sconce that needed no match or lighter. It had a twist knob directly at the bottom. I turned it, and the entire garden tool room lit up.

"Well, isn't that just the ace? What a shite," I couldn't believe my stupidity the first time around.

"Don't fret about it, Alister," Ned said understandingly. "Can't say that I would have thought about it myself," he hemmed and hawed, "er, if I found myself in your position, of course."

"So what now? Do we just sit and wait?" The room was filthy and didn't contain a single chair upon which to sit. "I had hoped my last encounter with that horrid creature was just a one-off. I really hoped not to see him again. Blimey." I realized I was making laps around the damp room.

"Well, we could call him." Ned chuckled. "Give him a yell. He might show up."

"Guess we didn't think too much ahead." On my current room lap, I passed by the brittle wooden door across the room from the hallway entrance. I stopped to look at it in the brighter light. I could see what appeared to be a plethora of crisscrossed markings, possibly caused by the continuous hacking of a knife or a hatchet against the door planks. Some were mere etches, but some were deep gouges that appeared to go halfway through the door. "Look at this, Ned. What do you think about this?" I stepped aside so he could see what I was looking at.

"Hum, I don't know." He reached out and ran his hand over the markings. "I didn't see anything about it in Randolph Junior's book." He pointed into one of the deeper groves, "Look here. Does that look like blood to you?"

"It sure does. I didn't see it in Randolph's book either. But the thing is, if Wilbur did this, why was he stuck in here? And look at this gouge. It is almost completely through the door. I didn't see these splinterings the first time I was here. But if he couldn't get through the door, he must have just gone back to the house using the hallway from which he came." Then I remembered. The newspaper had said they found him in front of this door, screaming like a blithering idiot and ranting on about ghosts. Exactly like me in front of this same door on Friday night. "Did he do this right before they found him?" I looked at Ned, "And if Wilbur did do this, then why wasn't it in Junior's book?" My eyes tensed, "Ned, that book even has our names in it."

"Right, you are, Alister. That I can't explain. But he didn't get through there, did he? Although, it seems Pat didn't stop him from trying either."

"And where is Pat? If he doesn't want us going through here, where is he now? Why isn't he trying to stop us?" I moved over to a row of shelves against the wall and began to search behind tools, pots, fertilizers, garden gloves, two walls fully lined with shelves of stuff.

Ned understood what I was getting at and helped from the other end of the second set of shelves. "Look, Alister, I didn't find any key, but I found this hatchet." He raised it above his shoulder and gave it a couple of swings in the air.

I hurried over to him and looked him in the eye. He handed the hatchet to me with a wink.

"No time like the present, I say," Ned chuckled. "If this doesn't cause Ole' Pat to show up, I don't know what will."

"Quite!" I ambled back toward the door and glanced around in anticipation of the horrific jeopardy I knew I was putting myself in. The memory of that bouncing clown caused my hands to begin to shake. I reached the door, put my hand against the splintered markings, and looked at the deepest gouge. "Well, here it goes." I lifted the hatchet and swung it with all of my strength. An agonizingly loud sound reverberated in that small room as I struck the brass hinge, and sparks flew from the blow. I shouted in shock from the explosion of noise in my ears.

Ned burst into laughter. And he did it again. He immediately eased the tension and the pressure that tried to stove in my chest. I bent at the waist and laughed with him. The fear and anxiety left me in a woosh.

"Well, that wasn't entirely what I wanted to do," I suddenly said solemnly.

Ned continued chuckling. He looked around the ceiling and yelled, "Did you hear that, Pat? We are going through this door," he looked back at me, "one way or the other, huh?"

With new ease, I lifted the hatchet again, and it fell directly into the deepest gouge. It only took three more swings to splinter the entire panel from the door. I reached through, turned the doorknob on the back side, and the door swung open with a rusty creek.

"Well, here we go. I guess the knob was frozen only on this side of the door." We picked up our flashlights from the metal table, which still housed the dreadful oil can, and stepped through the doorway.

The scent of stale moisture and mold assaulted us the second we crossed the threshold. The light spilling from the cellar reflected off a mist rising from groundwater, which was in motion and lapped softly at our shoe soles. I shone my torch on the floor in front of me, and we witnessed that the entire narrow room before us was a tunnel. Water seeped down the inside walls and pooled onto the floor to join the rising flood. Large stepping stones shone damp, mossy, and slippery in the beams of our flashlights. They were placed in a line from the door where we stood, straight across the narrow cavern floor, to where they ended in front of yet another door. Planks of wood interspersed the rocks where the gaps between were too far apart to step across with ease. It felt at least fifteen degrees warmer in here than in the cool, damp cellar.

"This is interesting," I said. "I mean, we know the water coming up from inside the caves scattered through this hill created the hot spring spas, but I had no idea that the caves would come right up to the house." I realized the mist rising from the water was not mist at all. It was steam. And the whiff of mold I believed I had detected could not have been. The water, at a steady one hundred and twenty degrees, per the brochures I read as a child about the spas, killed off any chance for mold or moss to grow. The water had to be cooled to one hundred and two degrees for the guests to be able to use the water pools. So, what looked like moss that covered the stones and walls had to be lichen. Lichen could thrive almost anywhere except entirely underwater. "Guess we better hurry through this part. I wasn't ready for a steam bath." A nervous chuckle escaped my lips.

I carefully stepped on the first stone, and the illusion of it being slippery faded as my foot found a solid purchase. I hurried over half of the rocks, then halted on a damp plank of wood, with which my feet found flat comfort, and turned to watch Ned. I visibly jumped to see him directly behind me, having chosen to fly rather than walk.

"Woah!" He said. "What did you stop for? I almost sailed into the back of you."

"Yeah, that was close," I said as he hovered slightly above my face.

A scream echoed off the tunnel walls, and Ned and I looked north across the cavern floor in front of us. The light from our flashlights did not reach the door at the end of the stepping stones. A vast and hideous grin blocked our beams, the nefarious toothy grin I had previously seen. The same copious amount of grotesque ichor drooled from between the teeth as I had witnessed previously. In my newly found fortitude, with Ned by my side, I was suddenly reminded of the Cheshire Cat, the moment he faded into nothing but his smile. The scream continued until I had to put my hands against my ears, flashlight pointed stabbingly at the cavern ceiling. My fortitude quickly dissolved, and my knees began to tremble. I inadvertently stepped off the wooden plank on which I had been teetering, and my foot plunged into the steaming water. Only a minuscule amount of boiling water spilled over my boot top. Yet, my immediate, shrill scream rivaled the one currently piercing my eardrums, and I pulled my burning ankle quickly from the scalding water.

My dear friend Ned scooped me up in his arms. We flew around the humongous smile that had suddenly sprouted a red bulbous nose and preposterously oversized oozing red-rimmed eyes. I'm not sure what was more dramatic, the greenish ichor drooling from between the teeth or the red brackish sludge seeping from the rimmed eyes that slid down the side of his nose and dripped off the columella nasi between his nostrils. A hilariously undersized green Irish tam perched askew on that enlarging ballooning head. The massive ball of a head began ricocheting from wall to wall in an attempt to block our forward movement. It might have been hysterically funny if I hadn't been so traumatized.

Ned counter-maneuvered, and we were around the bouncing head in no time. "Pat, give it up," Ned laughed. "I don't know what you are trying, but we know who you are and where you came from, and you are not frightening to us in the least."

Well, he could say that for himself. I did not find this funny at all. I felt the complete opposite. Yes, he was pretty damn scary. Ned could look at his silly little tam and giggle at his bulbous head bouncing around the dark cavern walls, but I was terrified.

"You sure might scare the kids," he set me down by the closed door that blocked our path, "But you sure don't scare us."

I wanted to spew the greasy stew. Yet I caressed the door in front of me. It felt smooth and freshly painted white, completely solid, cool to the touch, and did much to soothe me. I reached for the knob, and it turned easily in my hand.

"I wouldn't do that if I were you."

I looked back over my shoulder, and Patrick the Clown had morphed into his human, well, almost human, ghostly form. The cute, chubby, leprechaun-looking fellow with orangey-red curly hair, chubby pink cheeks, a sweet grin, and sparkling eyes.

"And why would that be?" Ned wasn't afraid to ask.

"You don't want to go there," was his reply.

"Why wouldn't we want to go there?" I found my nerve somewhere at the last moment. I guess it hadn't slipped too far away. "What is it you don't want us to see?"

"Oh, it's not me who doesn't want you to see." Pat floated closer to Ned, who stood gallantly between us. "Do you see that water going under the door? This little spring flows through the caves and down to the cavern hot pools, then past the hot pools and right into the theme park. And do you know what it does there?" Pat looked back and forth between Ned and I. It seemed he could see us perfectly well. Ned's and my torches shone the only light within the cave. And we both had them pointed at Pat, right in the old eyeballs. But I had no doubt he could see us as well as we could see him.

Ned glanced over his shoulder at me, and I shrugged. He turned back to look at Pat. "You've lost us, Pat. Who wants to keep us out of there, and what are you talking about with the water leading to the park?"

"Ned," I whispered close to him, "the door is unlocked. Give me a sign, and I can pull you though." It was getting pretty darn scalding hot, and with the steam and the fear, I had become soaked and uncomfortable.

"What say you, Pat?" Ned persisted. "You've told us nothing."

It dawned on me suddenly that we had to ask him about the children. The missing children. "Ned," I whispered again, "ask him about the children."

Ned looked at me and rubbed his damp, bald head. "Why me? Can't you ask him about the kids?"

He had me. I could ask as easily as he could, couldn't I? "Hey, Pat," I called around Ned, trying not to slip back into that steaming water."

"What do you want, Alister?"

"You know my name?" I was astounded.

"Of course, I know your name. Just like everyone else stuck here on Poland Hill."

"You're stuck too?" I asked incredulously. Why hadn't I thought of that? I thought Patrick was the one keeping everyone here. "I'm sorry, Pat. I had no idea. So what's the deal? Why are you blocking everybody else from getting to the amusement park? We read from a book Wilbur Hamilton found in the library that there is some kind of passage into the afterlife in the park somewhere. We deduced that you are the one keeping everyone from their final destinations. What do you know about that?"

Ned said, "Get right to the point, Alister?" He laughed.

"You wouldn't ask him. I don't like to beat around the bush."

Ned looked back at Pat, who now hovered right above us. "Yep, no beating around the bush. I'm not keeping anyone from their final destinations. I am keeping them away from the entity that has the children. If the parents, or any adult, confronted her, I don't know what she would do to the children."

"Who's her?" Ned wanted to know.

I wanted to know why Patrick was behaving nicely now. "Why would you scare them from getting to their kids?" I looked to Ned for reassurance. "I mean, shouldn't the adults even attempt to get the kids away from whoever she is? This lady or whatever?"

"Oh, she is no lady, Alister."

179

Ned and I looked at each other in the glow of each other's flashlights. "What do you mean she is no lady? Is she a ghost? Is that what you mean?"

Patrick floated down and stood in the water beside us. The water did not scald the nonliving. "You guys know Zeus, right?"

"Zeus, the Greek mythological king of the gods? I know him well from studying Greek Mythology at university," I was really confused about where Pat was going with this line of questioning. "But it is mythology. Correct?"

"I've heard of him too. I mean, who hasn't? He's even been in the comics, and there are movies about him. It seems like I just saw one right before my heart gave out." Ned agreed with me. "Oh, Alister. That's what happened. That's why I died. It was my heart! That is wonderful to remember." Ned actually did a little dance number perched on that wooden plank, water splashing up around his shoes, which, of course, didn't get wet.

"Well, that's good news, Ned." I slapped him on the shoulder. "Go on, Patrick. What does Greek mythology have to do with anything right now?" I said and looked back in his direction. Patrick wasn't there.

Somehow, he had moved between me and the white door when Ned and I got sidetracked by his little dance. Again, he blocked our way through. "Zeus had a daughter with Demeter. He was always messing around behind Hera's back. Hera was his wife and also his sister. And Demeter was also their sister. But Zeus was the king of the gods, so he could do what he wanted. Demeter was the goddess of agriculture, the harvest, and fertility, as well as the goddess of health, birth, and marriage."

"What are you prattling on about? Get out of the way. We are going to the park, and you can't stop us." I hiked my pants up higher, hoping I looked forceable but also just trying to keep them from dragging into the hot water.

"You see, Ned, Alister, Zeus had another kid with another one of his sisters. They were a strange lot, for sure. They named the kid Persephanie. She was a beautiful girl, as a goddess should be, I suppose."

"Patrick," I was getting irritable.

"Don't Patrick me, Alister. I'm Pat the Clown, remember?" He raised his hands as if to proclaim his title as worthy.

But I thought differently. "Oh man," I quickly conceded. "I don't want to see that again. You can be really disgusting."

Pat laughed, "You're darn right I can. Sometimes, I can be a not-very-nice man. Downright nasty if I want. Don't get me wrong." His head started to expand sideways and began to balloon up.

"I gotcha, I gotcha," I was not a wimp, but I certainly didn't need to see that again. My body started to shake in just remembering.

Ned reined us back in, "Guys, we need to get to the park. Go on, Pat."

"Well, gods being what they are, Zeus promised his daughter, Persephone, to his brother Hades. I know, right? Nice touch, dad! Give your daughter to your brother. So Hades kidnapped Persephone, and he made her his wife. Queen of the underworld. He made her the protector and keeper of souls. Strange job for a goddess who is also the goddess of the harvest, like her mother, Demeter. I have heard when Persephone is with Hades, Demeter mourns the loss of her daughter, the trees lose their leaves, and the fields dry up for the harvest. But when Persephone comes back in the spring, her mother rejoices, and the earth fills with regrowth, and flowers burst forth. I would think doing that to your mom might mess you up, even if you weren't married to your uncle." Pat shook his head but would not move from in front of the white door.

"So what does this Persephone have to do with the children, with guarding the passageway to the afterlife." I didn't understand. "How can she be the keeper of souls if she is Queen of the Underworld? Does that mean she is trying to take all the souls to Hades, to Hell? I don't get it." I didn't read anything about this in the library upstairs nor in the book *The House on Poland Hill.*

"You got me, pal," Pat answered. "I'm just telling you what I've heard. You know how ghosts gossip around here."

"Well, that's the first I have heard anything about all of this," Ned said. "But, I guess I've only been here six years."

I straightened my shoulders and took a step closer to Pat, who hovered in front of the white door. "So, the question here, Patrick, is whether you are going to help us or not? Are you going to try to help us get the kids and make sure everyone gets where they are supposed to go, or are you going to keep blocking us from helping all those fine folks back in the house." My mind returned full force to the pool house, horrid business, "and those fine zombies in the pool house?" I shivered in spite of myself. Then it came back, "And what about the hot spring that leads from the cavern pools into the park? What about that?"

"Yeah, Pat, you were going to tell us about the springs. Where do they go?"

Pat leaned in toward us to whisper. I don't know who he thought would hear him. "The gossip up at the house is the hot water leads right through the doorway to the afterlife and right down into Hades."

It seemed odd to see him shiver when he told us that. Ned and I looked at each other, and for the first time, we were speechless.

But the silence only lasted for a moment. "I love this old house and the library for sure, but I am ready to see where life is going to take us," Ned added.

Pat said, "Life? Where life is going to take us? I hate to tell you, pal, but you're dead like the rest of us." He reached up and wriggled his tam with a chubby hand.

"I know that, Pat," Ned answered. "I know that as well as you do. Do you want to stay here? Scaring people and other spirits for eternity? You've been here since what, 1918, right? It is now 2025."

It dawned on me that the construction of this house, the House on Poland Hill, was completed in September 1925. Exactly one hundred years ago this month. "You have been doing the same thing for over one hundred years. Is that how you like it?" I suddenly felt sorrow for Ole' Pat.

"You do have a good point. But no matter what you want or what you think, Persephone, the Queen of the Underworld, is still blocking the passageway to the hereafter. I don't know what you expect to do about that."

"Well, we aren't going to figure it out standing right here," Ned said. "Let us pass, Pat."

And to my astonishment, Pat stepped out of our way.

Chapter Fifteen

I opened the door. Ned and I stepped out of the cavern into the dusky evening. Something nagged at the back of my brain until I realized I was thinking that we had been in the same cave structure where the townsfolk had put Molly and her friends and then left them to die. I briefly wondered how Molly was fairing. Oh, right, she's a spirit, so I guess she is fairing well. She couldn't be worse. But they weren't, were they? The spirits. None of them. They were stuck on this damn hill for eternity unless we helped them. Angst tore at me to do something, but what could I do?

The door opened on the north side of Poland Hill, much further down than the pool house Ned and I had visited yesterday. This time, rather than staying behind as all the other spirits had done, Patrick stepped out of the door with us. It was still raining down sleet. I lifted my face, and it stung a bit. It hit my eyes and made them tear. I reached into my pocket to pull out a face tissue to wipe my eyes, then into my other pocket to pull out my mobile phone. That hand came up empty-handed. It was gone. I estimated that it was now probably about 10:00 p.m., and it was Tuesday night. I really didn't know for sure. It should have been pitch dark, not just dusk, at this time of night in late September. I needed to keep reminding myself what day it was, even if I couldn't remember the time. As I told you earlier, and as I kept being reminded myself, time was skewed on Poland Hill. Everything was skewed here, not just time. Nothing made sense.

In the duskiness of the evening, we could see the shallow natural pools littered the side of the hill where the rich and famous had come to linger and bask in the healing waters. In the bright moonlight, we stepped over the troughs that moved the water from the cave spring to the pools and started down the hill. I scanned the area around us. There were no flowers here as there had been yesterday. No Goldenrod, no purple Wisteria, nor wildflowers here. I could detect, through the fresh scent of icy rain, the smell of sulfur in the air. Sulfur, with the fetid stench of rotten eggs. My nostrils filled at once with the foul odor. It had not been present in the cavern tunnel. I wondered if this was what the smell of Hades might be. It was the smell of death. Had the Queen of the Underworld unwittingly brought Hades up to earth with her? My stomach lurched, and whether from the smell or the thought, I tried to chunder on the ground. Nothing came up. I attempted to remember the last time I had eaten, but the knowledge escaped me. But wait, it was only just this evening, about three or four hours ago. How odd. The wambling of my stomach protested otherwise.

We stepped onto a gravel path that led from the spa pools down the side of the hill toward the amusement park. The Farris Wheel, which I had seen from the mansion's tower spire, loomed larger as we descended toward the park. We were silent as we walked. The gravel path on which we trod turned and moved closer to the downhill stream. We found ourselves walking beside the growing body of water. It bubbled along, and I noticed it began to boil, the heat and steam rising instead of cooling as it traveled downhill. There was no way to anticipate what we were getting into. I was glad Ned and Pat had chosen to walk beside me. We moved at about the same pace. Pat was a little slower due to his slightly portly figure, but we were glad to have him with us. My fear of him had disappeared entirely. I had new creatures to worry about. Hades and Persephone? I couldn't even imagine that they were real entities, nor what other atrocities lay ahead.

We had not gone halfway to the park when we began to notice other spirits, other beings, slipping out from behind the trees, flying down from between the branches, and manifesting from behind large rocks. They came in all shapes and sizes, with the exception of children. There were none. Men and women, young and old, in various stages of decaying flesh. Broken bones, missing arms, missing faces. The burnt and the broken. Floating and hobbling as they merged behind us. A growing army of the dead. My own spirit swelled with courage as the forces behind us grew as the night descended upon us.

I looked up at the hotel perched atop Poland Hill. It was lit from within. Had I left all the lights aglow? I raised my eyes to the tower spire. I swear it winked at me. I rubbed my eyes to remove any hint of sand or dirt that might blur my vision. But when I looked again, the top window, the one I had looked down from to see the top of the Farris Wheel, the only one that could be seen by the townsfolk below, was afire.

Had Wilbur Hamilton known what he had written when he had written, "I can't do it!" on that page so prominent at the end of all of his griffonage? Had he known what event was unfolding here but had left us no message or hint of what we were to find? But he didn't have Ned and Patrick with him, did he? I turned from the hotel and looked at them moving beside me. My thoughts suddenly turned to Tom and Frank. Where were they? It had been days that I had been here, but they had not come. They had told me they would come that second day. Saturday it was. But they had not. Yet, as much as I wished they were here right now, I was grateful they were not. But what a story I would have to tell them when we finally met again. I smiled at Ned and Pat, and they both nodded back at me. We trudged on. I noticed that, at some time, it had stopped raining, and the sun had begun to rise.

Remember me telling you that time made no sense here? I digress yet again. But the darkness did set in, and the sun did rise as we walked down that north side of the hill. When the sun was in about the 9:00 a.m. position, the shadows of Poland Hill fell upon the amusement park and covered the rides in a shroud of darkness. The purpose of this ironic scene was not lost on me as we reached the edge of the park. The rides were all hidden from the glare of the sun. Had the architects planned this? Had it been intentional when the park was built here? We walked off of the gravel path and hit sand.

The park had been built entirely on sand. I didn't remember railroad tracks ever going through town, even in 1915. How did they haul it all here, I wondered? Yet, in the year 1914, the Japanese joined the allies in the fight against Germany in World War 1. They used sandbags around their trenches to protect themselves from enemy fire. Bullets couldn't penetrate the sand. And, from the town library archives, where I often spent summers in my childhood, I remembered looking at a newspaper, The Argus, from Melbourne, Victoria, Australia, which reported on Thursday, February 18, 1915, that the Hungarian troops fighting in Servia used beer barrels filled with sand to protect themselves from enemy fire. The men crawled on the ground and pushed the barrels with their heads to shield themselves from bullets. They also used them to roll along trenches for mobile protection against the enemy. And the Israelites built the great pyramids of Egypt, didn't they? It can be done. People always find a way.

The House on Poland Hill

We stepped onto the sand as the sun reached the high point in the sky, and the shadows slipped away from the top of the Farris Wheel, which was still quite a way off in the distance. It loomed mysteriously large to our eyes. It was about noon, solar time. And beneath that late September sky at noon, the typical temperature should have been in the mid-80s, yet it felt at least 110 degrees. The sand was everywhere, in all directions. Through the ages, the winds sweeping up through the Southern Live Oaks, Palmettos, and Red Oaks had blown in and caused the sand to invade every available orifice. As if on cue, the wind blew with just a hint, and the sand began to wisp in front of us.

We passed a carousel completely entrapped within a dune. Only the top of the domed roof and one horse head carrying a brass ring in its mouth stuck out from the misshapen heap. Ned and Pat opted to lift their feet from the ground and hover by my sides, the sand being too much trouble to bother with. I glanced behind us at the size of the growing mass of spirits. It had become a horde. The zombies had decided to join us. In a moment of panic, I realized, that very instant, that it was I, Alister Prescott, who was to be the one to save them all. I, who had to help them reach their destiny. And I was not worthy.

The size of the amusement park was enormous. One could not see the end from the beginning. There was no physical way the park had been built this big on the property located atop Poland Hill. It had grown and seemed to expand with every step we took. It must have been ten times the size of the house on the hilltop, which was no small fete. Dozens and dozens of rides and exhibition halls loomed before us as covered mounds of sand. It would take us days to find where Persephone had taken the children if that were the truth. I had my doubts about that story. And she would move them, wouldn't she? When we were near, she would move them, and then we would be forever searching. It was daunting to consider.

"Ned," I addressed the man on my left, the one who had once been my middle school history teacher, Ned Abernathy, once so young and handsome, now old, bald and dead, "Ned, what happens if we can't find them?"

"Oh, don't think like that, my boy! Why, look how far we've come." That was all he said. He turned his face to search the hidden, buried places around us.

I looked at the man on my right, chubby, pink-cheeked, red-haired Patrick The Clown, still in human, somewhat leprechaun unearthly form. "Pat, did you put an accelerant in the oil can you gave to Randolf Junior before the hotel fire? Did you start the hotel fire?" I had to know who was beside me.

He hesitated only a brief moment while he looked at me, then shrugged. "Not me, Alister. It was the house. Somehow, the house started that fire. But it could have been Hades," he shook his head, and the tam jiggled about but clung to his head. "One really doesn't know these things."

Well, that wasn't very clear. I was suddenly sure I would never know who started the Poland Hill fire.

The wind seemed to pick up a bit of speed, and the sand started to sting my cheeks slightly. Just like the sleet that seemed mere moments ago.

Then, Pat answered my previous question for Ned. "I think, and you understand I don't know much about many things, is to remember the gossip I told you about earlier. The bit about the stream, the hot stream, moving through the park and straight down to Hades, well, to Hell, anyway. I would think about that."

I hadn't realized we had moved away from the widening spring that was now a stream. I looked around quickly to locate it. "Patrick, you're right. How did we move so far from it?"

Ned overheard Pat's remark, and we all three started to search for the missing water. "I think we lost it at the carousel." He said nonchalantly. "I wonder how it would travel over this desert rather than soaking into it. Curious."

Had his sense of urgency left as it had yesterday before we found the pool house? What evil was at work here? Oh, yes. Pat had said it was Hades. I had not remembered Hades as a trickster from my Greek Mythology class at university. But he was the king of the underworld, wasn't he? My memory has always been a sure thing to count on. But, recently, I can't even remember what day it is. What day is it, anyway? I always thought Hades was an impulsive and deceptive fellow. Did he have anything with Persephone taking the children? Was she keeping them from him? Why would she take the children, to begin with? History told that she did represent spring and rebirth, fertility, and new life. Then I remembered she had no children of her own. What a juxtaposition for her. My mind whirled in circles, rambling this way and that, only to jump from thought to thought once again. I told myself that I must be vigilant and control my random thoughts.

I grabbed my wits about me and realized we had stopped our pursuit of the missing stream. The Carousel. We had to go back to the carousel.

Ned and Pat had moved closer together in flight. I ran as fast as I could, dodging around the stumbling horde who moved close behind and tried to catch up to them through the hot, blistering sand. I had been right earlier when thinking of it as a desert. The trees that had miraculously survived or escaped the fire, along with the new growth scattered through the park, had long since withered, dried up, and died under the onslaught of the desert sun. I realized that I wore no hat to shade my eyes nor my ascot to wipe the sand from my brow. My previously sweat-dampened clothes had long since dried and now, covered with sand, scratched my chest and back skin as the wind whipped past in a blast of arid heat. I never have, in my entire life, wished I were dead, but as I looked at Ned and Pat before me, floating effortlessly with the wind, not a care about the heat or sand, I could not help but envy them a wee bit. And I was thirsty. So very thirsty. When had my lips begun to blister? I would not be surprised if Ned was right and the stream had disappeared, sucked down into the dry earth.

I stopped a moment and used my teeshirt tail to wipe sand and tears from my eyes. I pressed the shirt to my eyes to give them just a moment respite from the wafting sand, and though the sun was high, the bright flashes of phosphenes were brighter still. I dropped my shirt tail and looked up to look for the guys. What I saw instead gave me great pause. I stood in the middle of the amusement park, in the middle of sand so expansive I could see no other ground around me, and a galleon ship sailed toward me and my following, burrowing a broad and deep trough through the sand in front of us. My mind immediately recalled my history class with Mr. Abernathy. We had learned of the fifteenth-century multi-decked ships, used as armed cargo ships and then as warships in the sixteenth century. Generally, built with three or more masts, these sails were raised against the wind. The desert winds blew the ships across the sand with the same ease as if they had been at sea. The captain and the crew aboard reminded me at once of the old movie *Jason and the Argonauts*. They raised their armaments high and shook them at us with skeletal arms, for they were skeletons. Not one ounce of flesh hung from their bones. They sailed past us swiftly and disappeared into the sand beyond us. They were gone as quickly as they had come.

I caught up with the guys when they stopped their flight above the carousel, then descended, alighting on the top sticking out from the dune. They looked down at the rambling stream bouncing along its merry way around the west side of the ride. It had grown in width, at least fifteen feet across, from edge to edge. It boiled along its journey across the park. I don't know how we missed it change direction or how we didn't see it from afar, although the wind eagerly swept the steam away as it rose.

"Well, that's it then," Pat said with his hands on his hips. "I guess we go that way."

I felt the mass of movement stumble in behind me. Would Ned and Pat believe me if I told them what I had just seen? I decided to wait until another time. A time when we could all sit back down in the library and talk about this when it was over. "I guess we do," I agreed. Oh, if I could have taken one moment to dig a hole out from underneath the carousel top and creep into the cool shadow hiding there, I would be blessed. I shielded my eyes to look up at the guys. The sun had moved further into the west. "Well, let's go then. What are we waiting for?" My voice belied not only my lack of strength but the sheer disbelief that clung to my brain, having seen that ship sail across the vast sandscape in front of me.

The guys took off, and the army of the dead began to move forward to follow by foot or by air. I stayed still for a few moments, still lost in thought, until I was behind a few rows of the deceased. I shook myself out of my stupor, and I prayed the creatures to my left would help block some of the rays of the sun from my weary, hot brain. If someone were to watch from afar, they would believe I was one of the undead, stumbling along, barely able to lift my feet as I plodded through the thick and sultry sand.

Chapter Sixteen

We continued following that blasted stream until it turned into a river. Then we followed it still. The moon had long taken the place of the blistering sun. And then, by the grace of God, it began to rain.

I raised my face and opened my mouth to the sweet, life-sustaining rain and used all of my strength and patience to let it pool in my mouth before swallowing.

I fell to my knees, surrounded by the horde. I swallowed mouthful after mouthful of sweet, pure rain. "Thank you, Lord," I began to laugh. The rain fell from the sky, backlit by the moon and stars, but no trace of rain clouds could be seen. A miracle, to be sure. But, as the horde and those I now called friends, Ned and Pat, watched in silence as I laughed, the rain began to pelt. And pound me, it did. The slight stinging of the ice and the sand paled in comparison to the barrage of the lashing rain. I jumped back onto my feet and shielded my face with my arms as I ran toward a massive dark hill before me. My once dry and raspy teeshirt clung to my body in the tremendous slapping torrent. I dove into the opening of an amusement ride and slid across the wet sandy flooring. I landed with a thump on my arse.

The opening of the amusement ride grew darker as the horde closed in the gap. I laughed. "I think I will stay here for a bit, lads and lasses. I am a bit exhausted, I'm afraid." I looked around for a dry spot and crawled over to the smooth, dry layer of sand. "I'll see you all in a little bit." I closed my eyes and slept.

When I opened my eyes again, the blasted sun was rising in the east. Was there to be no respite? I sat up to try to get my bearings.

"Are you better now?" Ned said from the ride seat he perched on beside me.

I jumped on my bum, having no idea he was so close. "Yeah, mate," I said as my stomach growled. "Unless you have an egg sandwich in your pocket, let's get on with it. I just needed a little downtime." I crawled out through the opening, not confident yet that I could stand, of what turned out to be a bumper car ride and looked at the sea of dead in front of me. More had joined as I slept. I also saw a few of the skeletons from the passing ship that had come. "Give me just a second," I said to Ned. Pat joined us, standing right behind me. I pulled myself to my feet and stepped around the dune to relieve myself of the rain I drank last night. There was not much to lose.

The river had grown. Again. Had there been rocks on the banks, I would not have been able to throw one across. We moved toward it, then turned north and followed it as we had before. But this time was different. I felt this day would be never-ending, rather than the dragging time yet quickly moving hours of yesterday. Did I previously explain to you that I never once questioned the river moving north? Rivers in South Carolina usually have a starting point in the northwest and flow southeast to drain into the Atlantic Ocean. I learned that little tidbit in fourth-grade science class. But not here. Not this one. And how did it start and end on Poland Hill anyway?

Well, we followed that river until my legs felt they were going to fall from my body. And just when I thought I couldn't take another step, the sun was now high again in the sky, and we watched as the river turned east. There rising in front of us was the Farris Wheel.

I looked up to where the sunlight shone upon the top of the amusement ride and could see the seats filled with children. The Farris Wheel was moving around and around, up and down. The excited squeals of children shrilled through the air, and for a brief moment, I forgot they were dead.

I watched those children for a long time. I know not for how long. The sheer joy of their laughter filled my heart with relief and with hope. Even if Ned, Pat, and I could not figure out how to open the door to the afterlife, we might at least be able to reunite some of these little ones with their parents. I watched that Farris Wheel circle up and down so many times I could not count, but then, the next time around, I saw it had caught on fire.

I tore my eyes away. There was nothing we could do for the little ones right now; they were already ghosts, and they were enjoying themselves, after all. Yet, if some of the children were here, then

Persephone would have to be nearby, so we kept heading the way of the boiling river.

We walked for what was probably only about ten minutes further when we rounded a dune, and the river moved into the mouth of an amusement attraction in the short distance and then disappeared. And when I say the mouth of an attraction, let me tell you, folks, that's precisely what it was. It was a funhouse. The doorway, if you can call it that, faced the east. The wind moved into the park from the west. Only the body of the amusement ride was deep within a covering of sand. The face was fully exposed to our view. The irony hit me and almost knocked me to my knees. One entered the funhouse through the big grinning red-lipped mouth in the face of a bulbous clown head. Ichor oozed out of those red-rimmed bright blue eyes. Green dripped from one nostril and oozed out from between his teeth. I was looking at Patrick The Clown. The ride, in big red letters, claimed to be "Patrick The Clown FunHouse."

"Well, I'll be. They made an amusement park ride of me!" Pat exclaimed beside me. "What'a you think about that?" He laughed in spite of himself. "I'm deeply honored." He actually bowed in my direction.

"Don't pat yourself too hard on your own back, Patrick." Ned admonished. "It appears you may have had a hand in this after all."

"I absolutely did not!" Pat became infuriated. "I had no idea they put this here. Why, how could I? I've been locked in that damn hotel for one hundred and seven years. And, if you recall, they built the park back in 1915. I didn't even know the place existed until I got here in 1918."

"Well, they must have added it after someone saw you in that damn cellar." Ned continued his attack.

"What are you getting mad at me for? I didn't have a hand or a foot or even my nose involved with this." He looked at the hideous grin, "though, I do think the likeness is amazingly well done. I'm actually looking at myself."

"Okay, okay. Just don't break your arm," Ned mumbled.

I listened to this exchange, and with my hands on my hips, all I had to say was, "Bloody hell." I had to deal with the damn clown again. I figured this monstrous clown balloon head would haunt me all my remaining days on earth, even after having come to a kind of friendship with the man, the ghost, Pat Monaghan.

"Yep, bloody hell," Ned mimicked me in agreement. "Well, here we are. No time like the present to get to it." He rubbed his bald head in the now blistering heat of the sun, but I knew he couldn't feel the heat at all.

We approached the horrid mouth, walking beside the rushing river. The river folded itself in half unnaturally lengthwise before it tumbled over the jutting teeth, plunged over a freakishly pink, spongy tongue, and down the repulsive yawning maw of the gullet. In the spaces between the narrowed river and the fat cheeks of the face, we found purchase. I stepped over the teeth and into the jaws of a nightmare. The sudden galloping of my heart and the all too familiar feeling and smell of icy tin in my lungs urged fear to settle deep within me. I self-diagnosed that I was reaching a state of dehydration. My pounding brain agreed with me. I glanced behind and saw the masses of broken men and women edging close to the ridge of gaping teeth. Those who stood, stood. Those who crawled, crawled. And those who flew hovered over the river. A horde of faces, burnt, torn, bloody, and oozing, stared after us as we entered the lair of the dragon. Hades was upon us. Would Persephone meet us at the door, or would we have to knock? Was there even an actual door? The book had said it was a door or passageway to the afterlife. We would know soon enough.

Having had enough forethought, we grabbed torches before we set off for the cellar. Was it just yesterday or the day before? It doesn't matter. We had them. Ned and I had carried them in our back pant pockets all of this time. So, we pulled them out and turned them on to light our way. I wondered then if Ned and Pat really needed the flashlights to see or if Ned carried it only for me. I would have to ponder that question later.

The temperature was tropical. The boiling river steamed up the walls. The spongy tongue gave way to solid wooded walkways on either side of a rail of seat cars. The cars sat rusted and frozen in place and time. No child rode these cars. We moved beside the train rail, holding the wall and the seats for stability, down the throat of the bogeyman as he floated in a false corporality beside me. A strange feeling, to be sure.

We moved slowly on the uneven walkway beside the train rail. Amusement rides always have walkways beside the rails to allow workers to enter for repairs, as well as rescue patrons in stuck rail cars. The funhouse was a conglomerate of rooms, each decorated differently than the last. I always wondered why they called them funhouses. There was nothing remotely fun in here.

The first room we entered was filled with moving, talking dolls. Another of my personal night terrors. They all began speaking at once. Blonde ones, oriental ones, a cowgirl atop a steed, ones with ball gowns and some in diapers, all heads turned simultaneously in our direction, "Alister, we have been waiting for you." "Alister, where have you been?" I felt my loin clinch and hurried through the moving, growing horror in an irrational fear. Monsters, whose painted eyebrows hovered over fiber eyelashes that fluttered over glass eyeballs of green, blue, and brown. Carved wooden or ceramic mouths that should not be moving nor able to speak.

Horrid dolls who tried to knock my feet out from under me and keep me there. "Alister, where are you going? You belong here with us. We will take care of you." Revulsion and terror stripped me of the last morsel of humanity clinging to my mortal soul. I couldn't help myself. I kicked them with my boots and set them sprawling and flying in all directions, only to have them crawl, broken and shattered back to me. I screamed. And I screamed louder and longer than that moment in the pool room when I first saw the zombies. Oh, yes, I did. The thing is, ghosts, spirits, vampires, witches, and even zombies had once been human in form. But these wooden, ceramic, and even plastic dolls, another obvious addition to the Patrick The Clown Funhouse since plastic wasn't invented when the park was initially built, these toys never, ever had a single living cell within them.

Yet, here they were, moving and talking and, I noticed, getting very angry at me. The entire floor, from wall to wall, moved with an unspeakable obsession to get to me. I looked down, and a redhead with freckles tiptoed toward my ankle, a five-inch steel knife held high above his head. It was Patrick The Clown. He was eight inches tall and wielded a five-inch blade. His balloon head was three times bigger than it should have been for a body that size. As his arm swung out toward me, Ned and Pat came to my rescue. They picked me up and flew me from that horrific place.

After the guys set me down in the dark tunnel, and let me tell you, I was loathed to put my feet on the ground, Patrick came to his self-defense.

"That wasn't me, Alister." He dabbed his face with his green jacket sleeve. "You know that wasn't me. I was right beside you all the time. I don't know who that guy was."

I bent over, put my hands on my knees, and breathed deeply two or three times to attempt to speak. My throat was raw from screaming. "I know, Pat. I know." But did I really?

We ventured into the next attraction room. Billowy, albeit grey, dingey, cotton sheet ghosts hung across the entire ceiling from ropes that allowed them to fly around above the heads of train car-riding screaming guests. This room was slightly comical, for I now knew what specters truly looked like. I had met not one soul who looked like a bedsheet. We entered a room set with several mechanical vampires drinking their fill from victims held within their sucking embrace. I lurched forward and started to run after one such creature released his lips from the neck of a young girl, and then he looked up at me and smiled. Blood trickled from his fangs and dripped onto his white linen blouse.

Although my stomach wambled, I felt no desire to throw up as I had almost every day since I had arrived on the hill. I felt a sense of accomplishment with that thought and straightened my shoulders. I was confident I was ready for the next barrage of my senses until I remembered those damn dolls and the palaver of their demeanor. They said they would take care of me. What a disingenuous, cunning disguise of their true motive. And what about that little Patrick? I shivered in spite of the blasted heat inside the entire funhouse.

We passed through a room that contained nothing but mirrors. Mirrors that made us look short and squat, then we passed ones that made us look ten feet tall. One mirror reflected what we looked like now, and I didn't recognize myself at first. A hairy, bearded face looked back at me. When had I become so thin?

We ducked and dodged many decades of cobwebs as we traveled through the belly of the funhouse. I was loath to think of living spiders dwelling here. But the cobwebs were long empty of their hosts, and I said a brief prayer for that. I knew a run-in with a spider would have been the last straw in my final grip on reality. We walked further than the park attraction was in length, supporting the fact that we were moving steadily down beneath the surface of the earth. As we followed the rail, it turned, rerouting its direction time and again, and although I became confused about which direction we were now heading, I knew, without a doubt, that we were moving toward the center of Poland Hill. Back in the direction from which we had come, directly beneath the hotel perched upon the hilltop.

Kathryn Cain

The ever-present river boiled and sputtered along beneath the rail platform. About the time I figured we were right beneath the hotel lobby, the tunnel in front of us began to glow. It wasn't a golden glow as one might expect from a lantern or lamp, but an eerie, foggy grey hue. I walked further in trepidation. My throat constriction withstood as we rounded yet one more turn. We entered a room decorated as the end times. The final destination, to be sure. The walls oozed a blood-red slime that seeped down and threatened to stain my already soggy boots. Fire leaped from the floorboards up the sides of the walls and skimmed across the top of the river as if oil had been spattered there.

The fire seemed to absorb some of the steam from the river, and although the heat was the most unendurable trauma I had witnessed so far, it seemed to take the moisture from the air and assist my breathing. What an odd conundrum. I didn't know fire could do that. But then I saw it. Right there in the very center of the room. The entire center of the room. The rail tracks, coming and going, were close to either side of it. Why hadn't I noticed it when I first entered this room? It was a replica of the Poland Hill Hotel. It was exact, apparent down to the tower spire, which reached the top of the room's ceiling. My hotel, complete with my auto, my cherry red Mercedes-Benz AMG GT C Roadster, sitting on the southeast corner parking lot, right where I had left it. I don't know how long I stood there staring at that hotel. The fire licking the walls and sputtering across the narrowing river crept closer to the replica. I noted the doorway to the Prancing Pony and saw to the west, at the fifth-floor level, there was no glass den attached there. Where had I spent the entire day yesterday? Was that just yesterday?

We exited that room and moved quickly away from the wickedness of the heinous goblins and demons who dwelt hidden within those rising and spreading fires.

We stepped back onto the slick, steamed-up, dampened walkway and back into the dark of the tunnel. We came around another bend and stopped abruptly in our tracks, hindered by a massive black wrought iron gate, yet it allowed the river to drop beneath the lowest bar and plunge to the depths of the middle of the earth for all I knew. The gate was engraved with the exact intricate scrolling design as the gate that crossed the driveway leading up to the property on Poland Hill Road. But it was not the gate nor the bubbling boiling river at which we stared.

On either side of the black-hinged gate floated an entity, each wrapped within layers and layers of copious amounts of delicate grey linen garments that billowed and fluttered in a non-existent breeze. The absent breeze caught up within their long grey, flowing hair and wisped it about their pale grey faces. Well, only their chins were seen. Their faces hid deep within grey-draped cowls like those I had seen in paintings of the Reaper. Twin beings of such voluptuous and complete grey beauty and grace I could scarcely breathe. Beings who were so effulgent I was afraid to gaze upon them and struggled to keep from turning my face away. It was not only their luxurious gowns of grey that moved so gracefully but the entities themselves. Their female forms, long flowing hair, and bodies' skin were the exact same pale glowing grey as their clothing. Their beauty was so exquisite my spirit welled up into my already constricted throat. I previously couldn't breathe, but I was now unable to utter a single sound. I would not have been a bit surprised to witness gossamer grey wings rising from behind their backs, and I fell to my knees in wonderment and awe. I forced my eyes to leave them and looked at Ned and Pat. They both stared at the embodiments of perfection in front of us.

Were they guarding this portal? Were they here to keep the dead from reaching their final destinations, or were they here to help us in our confrontation with Persephone or Hades? I had no words form about which to speak or ask.

"Rise, Alister," the entity on the left, the one closest to me, spoke. Her melodious voice did not move through the air from her mouth to my ear. Her mouth did not move at all. If it had, I could not have heard her over the thunderous roar of the river plunging below her billowing robes. I heard her in my mind and rose to my feet at once. I glanced at my knees. No fire-licked soot, water, or blood were saturated there. My pants were dry and clean, as if I had donned them only moments ago.

I felt at once like the cowardly lion meeting the wizard in one of my favorite movies. I wished I had a tail I could grab onto for comfort, and I used all of my strength to stand my ground and not turn to flee back from where we had come. In all my current days filled with specters, ghosts, zombies, and the like, nothing had prepared me for the beings who floated in front of us now. They were like pillars of truth guarding the passageway to forever after. Were they good, or were they evil? I felt in my heart that they were good.

The entity continued cutting through my wondering thoughts, which seemed to be the norm for my brain functioning of late.

"You may pass," she lifted one grey-sleeved arm and grey hand, her finger pointed toward the center of the black iron gate. Her twin had raised her opposite arm in silence and also pointed at the center of the gate. The gate swung open from the middle, twin gate doors for twin divine beings, messengers of a sort, but of whom?

Ned, Pat, and I took no time hurrying up to the gate, but I hesitated when I understood I would have to step into the fast-moving, boiling river, which tumbled where I needed to tread. Ned and Pat lifted their feet from the ground. Each grabbed me around my waist and floated me in through the open gate. We were loath to keep the apparitions waiting.

Chapter Seventeen

We floated over the river as it plunged to depths we could not see. The wooden walkway and train rail began again where the river had left off, and the guys set me down. The roar of the water was so loud I could not hear them speak. The greyish eminence from the twin oracles faded as we moved quickly away from the gate.

"Those were oracles, right?" I asked no one in particular. "Persephone, Hades, Greek mythology. Oracles were believed to deliver prophecies from Apollo. If I remember correctly." I was speaking so quickly that I hoped they could both hear me as the river noise faded in the distance. "Apollo, he was a son of Zeus. So Persephone is his sister. Apollo, one of his attributes is the protection of the young. His concern was the health and education of children. It is said he presided over the children's passages into adulthood. So, is he helping his sister protect the kids from Hades? What is going on here? And I also recall that Apollo had his sights set on Persephone before Zeus sold her to Hades. What a mess they had back then. But, why would Greek gods have anything to do with the people who died here at the hotel, or in the park, or Molly and her friends from the sixteen hundreds? Where are Persephone and her beloved husband, Hades, right now? And Apollo. Why are his oracles guarding that gate if it is the passage to the hereafter? Don't you think that it looked like the river leads straight down to Hell? Pat, just like you said, the ghost gossip suggested?" I was blathering.

"You got me," Pat answered.

"Yeah! Me too." Ned agreed. "This is definitely a new territory. I still can't get over the possibility of the door to the afterlife, any afterlife, is here on Poland Hill. Has probably been here all of my life, maybe for eons, and the entire town had no idea. I mean, how could we have known?" I could see Ned's thoughts spinning through the sudden absence in his eyes. He went on, "If the passage is here, then why am I the only one here from Prophet? Where is everyone else who I know died before and after me?"

His eyes glassed over again. It was just as well because I certainly had no answer to that. So I looked at Pat. "Pat, we are literally walking inside of your mouth and down your throat. Don't you think you would know something?" I said, and then I was quiet for some time. I thought about the little Patrick who tried to slash me, but I felt pretty bad saying that to him. I knew it wasn't his fault. I hung my head in shame, and empathy swelled within me. I finally apologized, "I'm really sorry, Pat. I don't know what came over me. I'm tired, thirsty, and worried about the souls imprisoned here, and I can't forgive myself for that outburst. I know it's not your fault, and there is no reason you should know what is happening here." I stopped moving and looked at him, floating quietly beside me. "There is no excuse. Please forgive me."

"Humph!"

I could see his eyes start to bulge, but just a little, and his cheeks turned scarlet. Then he picked up his speed and moved in front of me.

"Well done, Alister," Ned floated quickly after Patrick.

We pressed onward but moved silently through the rail tunnel as it moved ever lower below Poland Hill. I shook my torch a couple of times, sure that the battery was about to die at any moment. Yet there was just enough light to cast elongated shadows of myself against the walls. It was not lost upon me that Ned and Pat cast no shadows. My thoughts turned to the army of the dead. The ghosts, wraiths, zombies, those poor spirits in all stages of decomposition, waiting outside the big red clown mouth, in the blowing sand under the heat of the sun. And of the spirits of the children riding eternally around and around, up and down, on that Farris Wheel.

Was it such an awful existence after all? They all seemed happy to be where they were. But the welcome home party they had for me had told me differently. They confronted me and asked me to help them. They weren't happy there. They were trapped in the hotel and trapped on Poland Hill. And they hadn't even thought of the missing children. I had thought of them. Hadn't I? Well, that's why they followed me all the way here to the park, I suppose. I don't know how

I was able to help them leave the hotel or the pool house. But I did, and they had. And they were waiting for me to come back to them. Weren't they?

"You know those floating grey beauties guarding that iron gate?"

"Of course, Alister, we just saw them," Ned said.

"Well, they are Apollo's oracles. The one on the left, her name is Idalia. Apollo's half-sister, Aphrodite, was the goddess of love and beauty, and Apollo named the oracle Idalia after her epitaph. In Greek, Idalia means "behold the sun." The oracle on the right was Pythia, Apollo's oracle of Delphi." That was a strange thought, and I said, "But why is the Oracle of Delphi in Prophet, South Carolina?"

Ned looked at me with amazement. "How do you know all that?"

"They told me," I looked him in the eye, and he believed me without question.

"Well, what are they doing here?"

"They didn't tell me that part. I guess Apollo must be here."

I had not noticed the tunnel getting brighter as we walked. I walked. They floated. I was so lost in thought, so tired, until Pat started talking.

"Okay, Alister, I forgive you. But I deserved it. I scared you first. And I haven't really said, but I'm sorry about that too."

"Nobody deserves to be talked to like that. Sometimes, I am a bloody fool. You two are the best friends I have." Frankie and Tommy

214

crossed my mind but disappeared just as quickly. "And look there," I pointed ahead of us, "isn't it getting lighter?"

"You're right. I don't know why we didn't see it sooner," Ned turned his flashlight off, and he was glowing. "Well, I'll be damned." He raised his arms and looked at them. "What does this mean?"

"I think it means we're getting closer to the actual passageway to the afterlife," Pat looked down at himself. There was no glow radiating from him. "Oh, well," he shrugged his shoulders, "I could have figured that one out if I would have thought about it." He pretended to grin, but his head hung low.

"You don't know anything about what that means, Pat," I admonished. "None of us do. And we won't until we find Persephone, the supposed Queen of the Underworld, to find any answers." Then I thought about that. "Or Apollo, maybe. But I really don't want to run into Hades." I was gabbling again.

"Thanks, Alister," Pat raised his head and smiled at me. "That helps a lot." The red had left his cheeks, and they were pink once again. "I am right here with you."

I patted Pat on the shoulder.

He said, "You aren't glowing either."

"Hunh!" Isn't that true, I thought.

We continued our route, and I suddenly realized after we had gone several feet past the iron gate guarded by the oracles that the train rail had disappeared. It seemed we had finally left the actual funhouse, the part where the park riders were allowed to go. I should have thought of that back at the gate when the oracles had to let us pass through. I guessed the part of the rail that went through the gate was for maintenance. The riders could go as far as the replica of the hotel and out again. I wondered if the demons and goblins were there when the riders passed through or if they only arrived after the park was engulfed in flames. Or, maybe they were there only for the three of us. I supposed it didn't even matter now. Did it?

And though Ned was glowing, the tunnel itself was also getting brighter. This time, it was not a foggy grey illumination but a bright yellow glow as if it came from the sun. But as we were below Poland Hill, I knew that was not possible. Yet, I had seen a great many impossible things happening here. Hadn't I?

Ned seemed to be quite pleased with himself about the glowing thing. Pat was unusually quiet and did not tell Ned to be sure not to break his arm from patting himself on his back. That choice made me see Pat in a different light than before. He looked at me with those bright blue eyes and winked at me.

The tunnel had become a hallway, then became an entryway, and it opened up into the most beautifully ornate gold-filled room I had ever seen. While the lobby above ground was white and grey marble with etchings of silver, this room was ensconced in gold filigree. It was everywhere we looked. The room sparkled so brightly it was the emanation that glowed like the sun. I expected the room to boast decoration, chairs, and statues from ancient Greece. Hades, Persephone, and Apollo were Greek. However, the furniture was made in ancient Egyptian architecture and style. A throne in the center of the room would have been the perfect seat for a Pharaoh or King Tutankhamun himself. Golden statues guarded the room with the likenesses of Osiris, Anubis, Isis, Horus, and Set. However, the largest statue, placed in the center of the colossal room, was of Ra, the sun god who started all creation. He created and ruled over all other gods and the afterlife. It was before this statue that the golden throne sat. This throne was not the throne of a simple pharaoh or even King Tut. It was the throne of an ancient god. A god much older than the Greek stories of Zeus, Hades, Persephone, and Apollo. This room was not a room at all. It was a temple.

Between us, where we stood upon the threshold of the entryway staring in unabashed awe, and the center of the room, where the brilliant glare of the ancient statue near blinded us, ran the very river we had followed on this journey. It poured into the temple through a carved hole in the floor of the cavernous room and flowed from one side of the room to the other and down under the ground again. The water glittered under the reflected golden glare from the statue as if it were a false sun.

Now, I stood there, looking at that great hall of gold. Then, I looked at Ned and Pat, staring at the humongous amount of gold statues, trinkets, and the like, and wondered how far off and how wrong we were about the whole Greek mythology idea. I tried to remember where the thought even came from. I rehashed all the books from the library in my memory, all the books Ned and I had read and reread. None of them mentioned anything about any Greek gods. Poor Wilbur Hamilton had only scribbled about the clown. The only book that said anything about anything was the book about the hotel on Poland Hill, and the only thing that it mentioned was that there might be a doorway or passageway to the great hereafter. The Great Beyond. But nothing, nothing, had said anything about Greek mythology except for Patrick. The story came from Patrick in that dark, damp basement tunnel.

I looked at him and realized he really had offered nothing else in any way to help find the missing children, to find a way to help the hopeless souls find eternity. He had pretty much only floated beside me, watching what was going to happen. Pat turned to me and grinned. For an instant, that grin blew up into the gaping, oozing mouth that filled my nightmares since I first saw it down in the cellar. I don't know if it was my imagination or if it really happened, but I thought his eyes bugged out and grew a bit bigger looking at all the gilt before us. Then, like a cartoon character on the telly, his head ballooned up, and he began to bob up and down beside me. I stood rooted in place as if I had turned to stone.

I was finally able to turn my head back to look at the river. I thought of the two unearthly grey oracles at the scrolled gate who allowed us access to enter this temple. I knew oracles were elemental to the divination of Egyptian knowledge of the future and dream interpretation, including necromancy, the practice of communicating with the dead. It made more sense than the Greek god theory, didn't it?

Was I a necromancer? I had been communicating with the dead since the very day I arrived at Poland Hill. Is this what I am?

I sidled over to Ned. Ned, my middle school history teacher. The one who should have known about the history of Greek mythology and ancient Egyptian religion. Ned, who was always at hand, urging me forward. Forward to what destination? Ned must have known I was thinking about him because he turned to me and nodded. What was the nod for?

I suddenly felt alone. Even though Ned and Pat stood beside me, I truly was alone. I looked at the river, which still boiled along, and watched it combust into flames right in front of me. My face began to sweat. I did not know what would happen next. I thought about those broken and burnt, the army, the horde, including the zombies, who I was sure waited patiently for me outside the jawed opening of the funhouse. I thought of the children riding eternally up and down and around and around on that Farris Wheel. I stood there, knowing this had to be a horrible dream I was stuck in for perpetuity.

I also knew I had become undone. The last thread of my sanity was slipping away. And, as I looked at that boiling, flaming river, it began to flow red. It became a river of blood. I instantly knew what was to happen, and as if on cue, Ra, the symbol of the sun, creator of all things in Egyptian lore, rose out of the depths of the fluid. His back was turned to me, and he was clothed in gold with a gold leaf crown upon his head. Standing twenty feet tall with blood dripping from his bronzed flesh, he turned and looked down at me. I fainted dead away.

You look at me now. Judging me. I know you are. You ask me what happened to the children, to the broken and empty souls I was to lead to their eternal home. I don't know the answer to these questions. I will probably never know the answers.

I woke to the sound of someone banging on the ten-foot-tall twin mahogany hotel doors and the sound of splintering wood. I roused myself from the sofa I found myself upon, and I could hardly lift a foot, but I found my way to those huge doors and the incessant pounding that matched the pounding in my brain. I saw my hand reach out and grasp the blackened brass lock switch and handle of the door and pull it inward as an axe head splintered the wood beside my face. There, on the stoop in front of me, my old pals Tommy and

Frankie rushed in, jabbering so intently I could not grasp what they were going on about. There were three firefighters with them, axes held aloft. And, my God, Mrs. Wintergreen was standing behind them, her hands held up to her face in shock, "Oh, don't damage the doors! Those lovely doors!"

I looked at my friends, my mates, with wonder. Where had they been these many, many days? Why were they not here to help me in my plight with the lost souls? I needed them here with me but had endured it alone. I had not remembered them as I saw them now. Middle-aged gentlemen of similar stout stature, I saw the boys of yesteryear. My mates of twelve years old.

I realized at that moment that I always thought of them as twelve-year-olds. Forever in my mind. I was twelve once again. They ran in the doors and grabbed my arms as my legs collapsed beneath me and saved me from hitting the floor. I heard hints and pieces of words. "Alister, we have been trying to get ahold of you for three weeks. Where have you been? Why haven't you been answering our phone calls?" Then Frankie said, "Oh, my God, Alister, you look like you haven't eaten since you've been here. And what is that stench?"

Tommy shushed him and said, "Ali, we're here for you, buddy. We will take care of you, pal. We're going to get you to a hospital."

I tried to open my eyes as I listened to the voices of my mates, Tom and Frank. The only thing I heard myself say, over and over, was, "I can't do it. I can't do it. Hamilton was right. We can't do it." But I had made it further than Hamilton, hadn't I? He hadn't gotten past that cellar door.

Those firemen took me out on a stretcher, blathering just like old Wilbur Hamilton. I knew I was safe. Yet, fear surged in my chest, and my stomach lurched. I wanted to vomit by the sheer thought of what I had seen, what I had witnessed. My mind and my eyes were filled with a terror so profound I will never forget it. The horror, the revulsion I will live with to the end of my days. The monstrosity of the weight I feel for not guiding them to their final destination has become an eternal part of me. I loathed to accept this as my fate but was unable to make any other sense of it. It has always been my destiny to end up in this hotel. The truth of it hit me then as solidly as the fear itself. I will carry this truth and this loss within me until my last breath. I curled myself up on that stretcher into the smallest ball my body could make, and I wept.

They loaded me into the back of the ambulance and drove out of the parking lot, past my Roadster, and onto Poland Hill Road. I opened my tear-streaked eyes, my face haggard, bearded, covered in soot, and I looked out the back window at the house, at the hotel.

I swear to you, now, as I sit here rationally, telling you what happened last fall, when I looked out the back window of the ambulance at the hotel, that window, the one at the top of the tower near the spire, it winked at me. I knew it at that very moment. I am a necromancer. I talk to the dead. And the house wants be back.

The End.